Ladies' Own Erotica

Ladies' Own Erotica

Tales, Recipes, and Other Mischiefs by Older Women

THE KENSINGTON LADIES' EROTICA SOCIETY
ILLUSTRATED BY PAT ADLER

TEN SPEED PRESS
Berkeley • Toronto

Any similarity to real persons, places, and events is in the eye of the beholder.

1🌀

Ten Speed Press
P.O. Box 7123
Berkeley, California 94707
www.tenspeed.com

Distributed in Australia by Simon and Schuster Australia, in Canada by Ten Speed Press Canada, in New Zealand by Southern Publishers Group, in South Africa by Real Books, in Southeast Asia by Berkeley Books, and in the United Kingdom and Europe by Airlift Book Company.

Library of Congress Cataloging-in-Publication Data on file with the publisher.
ISBN 1-58008-395-1

Cover design by Jennifer Barry Design
Text design by Nancy Austin

Original printing 1984. Reprinted 2002.
Printed in Canada.

2 3 4 5 6 7 8 9 10 – 05 04 03 02

We affectionately dedicate these pages
to the memory of our patron saint, Judd Boynton.

—*The Kensington Ladies*

*Here are a group of unassuming women who can teach us
men much. In their statement addressed to penis owners
there is a significant lesson . . . a profound insight that men
will do well to read . . . and re-read . . . and profit from.
But there is more . . . much more . . . in the tender art and
sensual joy of love and sex. It is much more than fucking.
Much that men can learn from these women, and tens of
thousands like them across the nation, if only we will take
the courage to put aside our macho arrogance, and learn
to touch and feel and ride with pure emotion. Let us men
take up their challenge and make the sexual revolution
complete.*

—Judd Boynton

CONTENTS

VI. GAMES WE PLAYED

VII. THE KENSINGTON LADIES REVEALED

VIII. A PROPOSAL

INTRODUCING THE KENSINGTON LADIES

We are an improbable group of women over forty, for whom dashing off an erotic story was one more task to be sandwiched in between trips to the supermarket and visits to the dentist. Some of us scribbled erotic tidbits on the backs of envelopes during lunch hours while others lavished whole weekends on a story. We regard ourselves as women who embarked on an experiment and, as a kind of afterthought, wrote and published. We met at one another's houses, prepared and ate hellishly good meals, and confided our sexual fantasies like pajama-clad schoolgirls.

It was Sabina who, seven years ago, gave birth to the group. Always the instigator as a child ("I'll be the witch and you..."), her questions to us were: Do you think women and men agree about what is erotic? Are our experiences different from theirs? Do we really know what turns us on, or do we just go along, accepting and acting out what male writers proclaim to be erotic?

Our first meeting, a potluck dinner, was at Sabina's house. Only a handful of women came—not quite knowing what it was they were coming to but clearly pulled in by the word "erotica." Right off, we discovered that we shared an unbridled passion for food. To establish a feeling of safety, Sabina assured us that this was not to be an encounter group and that no private revelations were demanded. We then took a dutiful look at Anaïs Nin, Henry Miller, and Nancy Friday and even glanced at the technicolored vaginas and muscled playboys of *Penthouse, Chic,* and *Playgirl*. We were not aroused!

Our writing began, at Sabina's instigation, as an "assignment." Drawing on our love for food she asked, "If you could concoct a recipe for a perfect lover, what ingredients would you use?" (For many of us cooking has always been a safe expression of our erotic selves.) In response we turned to our adolescent awakenings, then to our movie star idols from those years, and finally to enchanting strangers from exotic lands. These confrontations reminded us how seductively we had been sold on women's helplessness and victimization. Out of this recognition came our one rule: no victims. Our efforts to shelve sexual stereotypes have not always worked, but as we became more aware we were able to play with them.

We continued to meet every month. Each home was different, but the ritual remained the same. We began our Erotica evenings with chilled wine and, of course, hors d'oeuvres: crackers, sly and salty, crusty French bread still warm from the local boulangerie, Brie spreading dreamily across the cheeseboard to mingle with the sturdy Gouda and the owlish Swiss, smoked salmon, rosy and pungent, and black olives glinting with a hint of malice from a glass bowl. Like ceremonial swords, these offerings allowed us to carve out the slice of time we needed for transition.

The presence of our men at these preliminaries added a particular flavor. The resident husband or lover, by mutual consent, was there at the outset—graceful, suave, polite, supportive—but, we noticed, his knuckles tight on the wineglass stem, the area about his mouth a little drawn. We would smile, loving smiles. We would grow remote, eager for the coming experience. We felt ourselves slipping beyond a tangible boundary: we were mysterious, powerful, eminently desirable—ready to cast our precious domestic bread upon the wine-dark waters of our fantasies.

And then the moment arrived, exquisite, wordless, inexorable—the moment for the man to withdraw. And that was when the fun began! Erotica!

I. AWAKENING

*R*eminiscing about our sexual awakenings, most of us recall a vivid time that passed with glacial slowness. We gathered information randomly—poring over pulp magazines, clandestinely comparing our anatomies, blundering in upon lovers locked in stolen embraces, or overhearing conversations not meant for our ears. We consulted the dictionary, which thwarted our search with rebounding synonyms and glaring omissions. We puzzled over the meaning of ambiguous phrases like "he took her" or "she came," knowing there was more to these familiar words than we understood.

Our awkward revelations left us unsettled and aroused. We took our cues from friends and older relatives and learned to disguise our naïveté with sophisticated trappings: stockings, lipstick, earrings. We spent eternities sunbathing, shampooing, grooming for that first kiss. What a relief when it finally came, even though it fell far short of the delirium of "movie star kisses"! In the recollections that follow, we allowed ourselves to be carried back into childhood's sensual drift.

Summer Rain

There are experiences that have no age, even when the people in them are children and one of them is you. The image remains with you just below the conscious level, and nothing that's happened to you since in any stage of love seems to equal it.

A summer rain in the dry San Gabriels causes a lot of excitement. The dusty pine needles drain off into powdery earth, and there is the expectant feeling of a very special event; even the smell is special. I am in a cabin in those mountains when the rains come, and I am thirteen and in love with a genius of fourteen. Of course his family is there with us, and I'm their guest, so I hide my feelings.

While the rain falls, sentimental songs play on the ancient phonograph. The words are as foolish as the mannered voices singing them, but the word *love* occurs frequently, and it has recently become a powerful word to me. So I gaze dreamily away while everyone else is laughing at the quaintness of the music, and they tease me about it. I long for older times when thirteen-year-old girls were thought marriageable women although they could be dead in childbirth at fifteen. That short, intense life could be richer than dreams of roses, but I'm expected to live a long time and not to discover my sexual self for many more years—maybe when I'm twenty-one it's supposed to happen—and at thirteen that seems like another century.

In the stormy evening when his parents and his sister go off to bed one by one, leaving us to lantern light and the fire burning down to glowing ashes, our eyes want to meet and detonate the charged air. But we are both suddenly afraid of something, so we agree without words to dance. We dance very well together as a result of our lessons, and we take pride in that, careful not to let it degenerate into an embrace. Still his fingers at my waist feel like misplaced fireplace coals, and when the phonograph winds slowly to a stop, neither of us moves to rewind it. The rushing of the rain water down the dry gullies outside is now very loud. All the earth's messages seem to tell us to come together, and our eyes finally engage in that long-deferred glance.

But there are stirrings of late-night activity from the family, and we are reminded that the planet is not solely our own. A spark has fallen on the Navajo rug, and I rush to put it out while he restores function to the phonograph. The electric moment is gone.

We make hot chocolate and discuss the meteorology of the rainstorm. After all, he is a science prodigy, and rain cannot be regarded as merely romantic. The phenomena of nature occupy much of our daily discussions and contemplations, believing fervently as we do that everything man can perceive in the cosmos will someday be understood. When we are both very sleepy, we part at his bedroom door, and our goodnight kiss is as soft and sensual as it is brief. Even young love wearies and needs rest more than fulfillment.

When I awake alone and lost at 3 A.M., I know something cataclysmic is happening. There is a dense blackness and silence in my room, but I'm sure some sound awoke me. Then I feel the earth buzzing and humming through the planks of the floor, up through the old iron bedstead and into my very bones. There is an immense crackling sound and a sizzle of the most intense light I've ever dreamed of: every object in the room has its halo. Instantly, a roar of sound shocks my bed and floor and room and roof. Outside, crashing reverberations roll up and down the mountainside and out into the valley, echoes reinforcing echoes.

I am terrified and fascinated and leap out of bed to witness this judgment day, padding barefoot to the window. As I stand there in my child's pajamas, which have somehow crossed over into my adolescent wardrobe unnoticed, I am suddenly aware of someone behind me. I'm prepared for a ghostly presence on this night, but it is a familiar newly deep voice that whispers: "Lightning may have struck the cabin—there was no time-lapse before the thunder." His arms come around me, and his dear warm body snuggles against my shivering frame. There is a long wait for the consequences of either the lightning or the illicit embrace, but nothing happens. "Let's get into bed—you're cold," he whispers.

Without another thought the icy bedsheets are breached, and we lie shivering together in the tangle of old wool blankets and tired feather pillows. Once only we look toward the door—it is firmly closed and bolted, and no further thought of intrusion crosses our minds through the rainy night. Our total embrace of arms and legs, cheeks and temples, hands and hair, begins immediately. The comfort of our mutual presence is overwhelming. My seizure of shivering stops, and a sweet warmth begins to spread.

The outer storm still crashes, but it is less threatening now, moving slowly along the mountain range and out into the valley. Our lips touch and draw apart. "You know we will not do the corrupting things," he says. We know, because we have discussed it long and philosophically: love is the universe and its suns; lust is the dark side of the planets. We are not sure how the drenching desire we both feel fits into the cosmos, but we know it must have a place this side of corruption. We trust completely and that trust cannot be betrayed.

As the hours pass, we lie entwined, shifting slightly for comfort, pajamas unbuttoned so the warm flesh of each embraces its counterpart. There is drowsing and waking and drowsing again. Lips brush and cling in infinite kisses. Tongues flicker over eyelids and earlobes and touch tongues. Toes caress toes. Knees and arm joints work past each other to meet at smooth places. Hands cup and fondle. His arousal brings my fingertips to stroke and release. His fingers run the rapids of my warm caves and hollows, lingering while I lapse into sleep. We awake to resume the caress interrupted by sleep.

When dawn lightens to gentle shades the storm is only a faint echo in the far distance, and our own world is dripping, quiet and serene. For a long time I watch his dear face sleeping, then slip into sleep to wake and find him watching me. Then suddenly he is disentangled and gone.

Now I sink into the sound sleep I had not had all night, and it takes the whole family surging in my door at ten o'clock to awaken me. Only one question is asked: "How could you sleep through that incredible storm?" And "Ahhh, to be young!" from his mother.

Later I learn that we had experienced a landmark summer storm for those mountains, one which became local history of fallen trees, crushed cabins, and washed-out roads. But in my personal history the image remains of embraced bodies, a depth of closeness in our intertwined forms, the absolute trust and visceral intensity of our happiness together. Long after I've forgotten how the love ended, the memory keeps an ephemeral presence that mocks all future moments of abandonment and ecstasy. Nothing, nothing, has been like that summer storm at thirteen.

Retreat

He stalks the corridors of the school, a magnet in black Jesuitical clothing, virile, comminatory, physical, remote. Terence Trumpington, S.J.,
visiting priest to the convent where I am being educated: celibate, sexual, imported from God knows where to guide us—two hundred reluctant virgins, ages thirteen to seventeen, and our fragrant, fluttering potpourri of wimpled jailers—through this year's Retreat. For six days we
withdraw from the world of schoolbooks and schedules. We embrace
prayer, silence, meditation. We confront our souls. The younger pupils
and that race apart, the "non-Catholics," inhabit a parallel pedestrian
universe. For them, business as usual: black marks, blotters, rule and
rote. For us the devout, the white-veiled, life has become the realization
of a page torn from an illuminated manuscript. We are lambent, we are
sanctified, we are obsessed. We are a group of willing sacrifices. Since
the initial shocks—his white-blond mane like deadly exposed wires, his
voice, his resonance electrifying out liquid flesh—we are ready at the
flash of a blunt white hand to hang up our girdles on the nearest bush.
Every one of us, now, answers to the name of Heloise, hears the name
whispered like a summons down every corridor of vaulted dark. Drawn
by invisible gold threads, which he holds in his hands, we are tugged
toward him into his magic circle of mystery. He is a charmed particle in
our shadowy, flickering universe of rules. Normally, we rarely see men;
those we do see have already been transliterated and have lost their
enchantment. They are flat cutouts of their particular functions: gar-
deners, altar boys, visiting siblings. Occasionally, one of us will roll up

her purity into a tight ball of rage, hurl it in a high arc across the pierced light of a painted window, and get pregnant.

And now, among us, is a most passionate priest. Padding across our hidden consciousness, he is tawny, magnificent, feral. He circles us, growling softly, brushing our skins with exhalations that have the same blood scent as the flood of our own moontides. His movements are fluid, released in distributed tension along his limbs and throughout his body. The early sun strikes bent bars across his brow at mass; his vestments flash like jewels, like plumage; his body snaps the brittle morning air. He crackles; bowing, bending, spinning, he performs before the tabernacle his love dance to our waking souls. Later, in his talks with us, his sensual intellect splinters like gold leaf the sequestered, swooning chapel air. Soft now, the air, and pliable; the incense hangs in stale tatters above our heads. Breathing the brocaded atmosphere, refulgent, odorous, we sense our suffocation amid white waxen flowers and votive lights that flicker crimson in their pots of oil. We watch the flames dancing on fat thrusting candles and feel the aching weight of burgeoning breasts that throb, rosy and tumescent, beneath our stout viyella blouses. Our veils bestow a furry bloom to our hair; every shrouded cheek holds the pale polish of desire, reflected in the snail-track smears we find each night on the cotton crotches of our panties. Some of us are menstruating; the rich marine smell of monthly blood communicates our restive longing, and our periods spread like a medieval mania as we watch our fantasies take shape behind bound volumes of *The Live of the Saints*. Orgasmic Theresa, drooling Damien, raving, quivering John of the Cross: our thighs are sticky with the fluids of our crepuscular dreams. Possessed, our lives saturated by our moist imaginings, we move uneasily on our hard wooden benches. From the swollen convolutions of our sex slide the glistening, undulant whorls of our desire. Carnal longing crawls from our groins and, groaning, prowls restlessly in search of Terence Trumpington, S.J.

Imperceptibly, we have changed. We are alien and suspicious, haughty and challenging to one another. The schoolgirl canter along the corridors has slowed and stopped; now we flow from the base of our spines, arm slack in rhythm to the superb pelvic sway. We ripple; we surge with high breasts and throats arched. Our breath comes hard; in our nostrils we feel the tight dry tingle of desert air; we follow the rumor of the crowd, swarming barefoot along the Way of the Cross in pursuit of the sweating, bleeding figure in the scarlet dust ahead of us. And our Magdalene hair, red and rampant down our backs, lifts and stirs in the sour yellow breath of a Galilean afternoon. We follow our lover over rocks and bones to the place of the stark triple trees, and we are gulped like draughts of air and water into the cavern behind the rolled-back stones.

Alone with him at last, dusky, murmuring; lips a whisper away from his ear, from his hand resting against a pallid temple. Like a stripper he will see my soul, he will look at me at last. A touch, just one touch! Like this, below the belly, where the pubis thrusts out curling copper tendrils (ah!) and here, on the nape, quickly, between the braided ropes of hair (ah!) and down over the shoulder, between the breasts, here beneath the jutting stone . . . There's time, yes, there's time, before it's all over and you have to go . . . I will hold you softly in my hand, like velvet, and lick the shiny dewdrop from the tip, like this. Ah, love, now you're nailed, expiring with a scarlet wound. They've stripped you to a loincloth, but I will draw it aside, like this; I will join you on your gibbet and straddle your body and slowly change the groans that wrench from you to murmurs of ecstasy . . . *Agnus Dei, qui tollis peccata mundi,* don't let me die, touch me, save me. Sweet cleric, leaning across the altar to pronounce the darkling words of the Transubstantiation *(corpus Domini nostri, Jesu Christi),* I have stripped you of every stitch, all off, chasuble, stole, alb, soutane, stripped you to your loincloth and bent my face to your groin, inhaling the scents of yeast and leaf mold.

"Have you committed any sins against purity, my child, in thought, word, deed, or omissions?" *Mea culpa, mea culpa, mea maxima culpa:* impale me, my censored one. I shall unfold to you, petal by petal, a veritable rose of sins. I pass before you in my veil, murmuring my trespasses into your dusky confessional ear. Body and blood; body and blood; my adolescence drips from me, pricked by crimson thorns; roses burst from the nail wounds in your feet, and I pluck them and wind them in my long red hair. *Et te, Pater:* inhale me now, as you ponder my penance; bless my petals, my vices, my inward, salivating womanhood just recently declared in blood. *"Ego te absolvo."* Am I dying? "Go in peace, my child, and sin no more." I smell of earth and flowers and sweat and dew; and for gazing with impurity upon the crucified figure of Our Lord, Terence Trumpington, S.J., stern, austere, glittering with the white light of grace, pronounces sentence: three decades of the rosary and twice around the Way of the Cross. We are dazed, vacuous, blundering into one another, for the chapel is very crowded this Friday afternoon. Oh Father, forgive us, for we know now what we do.

Bedtime Story

I can still see the three narrow beds, each with a chair at the end where our underwear is neatly folded beneath our skirts, our blouses draped smoothly over the back. After thirty years I still shiver when I remember that unnerving coolness that clung to the bare white walls even in summer. It had nothing to do with the climate, but with the absence of love that left me terrified from the moment my parents abandoned me at my aunt's house.

"It will be good for you to live in such a large family," they said in parting. I violently disagreed. There were four boys and two girls. Although Sigrid was ten like myself and Ursula only a year older, I did not know my cousins well. The girls wore identical dresses, and even their shoes and socks matched at all times, for my uncle owned the clothing store on the ground floor of their rambling old house. My parents had told me about their good manners and about the discipline that my aunt and uncle exercised in running both store and family. "They will teach you to keep order," said my father, who thought that my mother had spoiled me while he was away in the war.

I soon learned that the store was the heart of the house; it compelled everyone to live by the hours it opened and closed. We children received our orders at breakfast, and every chore was checked on schedule by Tante Gerda, whose eyes were everywhere. Although she never punished me for my negligence, I was terrified of her.

I was also terrified of the dark and of losing my mother. As soon as I closed my eyes, I would imagine all kinds of things that might happen to her. Ever since the bombing of our apartment house, I was afraid of airplanes. I dreaded that she might get hurt by an airplane or by falling out of a moving train. Every day on the radio the Red Cross listed the names of all the parents and children who had lost each other. I imagined the crowded train and my mother telling me to hold onto her hand. But then somehow I had to let go, and she fell out.

I wanted to read before going to sleep, but Tante Gerda did not allow us to turn the light on. My favorite book was *Arabian Nights*. She took it away because she found it unsuitable for children.

I marked my calendar, counting the days until my mother would return. "I'll be back in time for your birthday," she wrote. But then she sent a telegram that she could not get away. My father was still looking for a place to set up his business.

"She promised to be back for my birthday," I cried. My cousins teased me that she would never come back and that I would have to stay with them forever.

"Now, now, one might think you are homesick," frowned Tante Gerda. She was the only person in the house who did not know that I cried every night. Even Onkel Johann occasionally brought me a piece of candy to help me go to sleep.

On my birthday he pulled a handful out of his pocket, but I pushed him away and flung myself out of the bed toward the window. I banged against the shutters screaming: "I want to get out of this prison! I want to get out of this prison!" They all came running, Tante Gerda, the boys, and Anna, the maid, who took me in her arms: "The poor little dumpling; I know just how she feels." Anna too was homesick for her native Rumania where people spent all their life dancing and kissing. Tante Gerda insisted that Onkel Johann should give me a spanking, but he gently picked me up and carried me back to bed. Then he shooed the family out of the door, proving that he was after all the master of the house. Sigrid and Ursula were enthralled. I had finally won their admiration. "She'll punish you tomorrow for sure," they agreed. I didn't care. I knew that I had to stop crying. I decided to try to keep myself from thinking about my mother.

"You want to hear my story from *Arabian Nights*?" I asked. "It's about Harun-al-Rashid and the slave girl Suleika. It's a forbidden story."

Naturally the girls wanted to hear it. Like Scheherezade, who kept alive by telling the story every night, I managed to keep myself from crying night after night as I cast my magic spell over Sigrid and Ursula. They even joined my game eagerly when I suggested we act out our stories. Sigrid was the new slave Suleika, and Ursula the sheik's favorite wife Rahmoon. From then on I was no longer a scared little girl but the mighty sheik Harun-al-Rashid.

We began with Suleika dancing the dance of the seven veils. While I told the story, she removed them one by one: first the brown, earth-colored veil signifying that she was a slave, then the orange veil that revealed her noble birth; the blue veil showed that she was a virgin; and the red veil told about her joy of becoming a woman. Finally, only the gold veil covered her skin because gold was the color of a royal harem. In this veil she danced her bridal dance while the other wives beat their cymbals and tambourines. Many of the wives hoped that she would make a wrong move and be sent back to the orphanage, especially the sheik's current favorite, the clever and beautiful Rahmoon, who had not yet produced a son and needed to keep Harun-al-Rashid's nightly favors. But Suleika danced perfectly until she fell exhausted to the ground.

"I shall visit her tonight. Bathe her in donkey's milk and rub her with oils and perfume," ordered the sheik.

"But I hoped you would spend the night with me," chimed Rahmoon. "I have prepared a special dance for you." Only his favorite could dare to speak without asking for permission, but Harun-al-Rashid allowed her to perform for him. She moved so seductively, shaking her diamond bracelets, that he once more succumbed to her spell and promised her the night, but not until he had greeted Suleika, the newcomer, as befitted a noble sheik.

When I crossed the room to Sigrid's bed, my bare feet did not walk on linoleum but on marble. My pajamas were studded with diamonds, and Sigrid's nightgown was a golden veil. Gently, I touched her face and removed the last veil. I told her how beautiful she was and how she must not be afraid because from now on her life would be given only to dancing and loving. Suleika remained still, but when Harun-al-Rashid took her into his arms, she nestled closely against him.

"I will now make you a woman." I pressed my naked belly against hers. Shyly, she felt my buttocks, and a warm glow spread from my secret place between my thighs urging me to explore her forbidden parts.

"Open your loins for me, sweet love, and receive my seed, the seed of the royal house of Rashid."

"I hope it will be a prince like you," whispered Suleika.

Then I hurried over to Ursula's bed.

"I kept my promise, favorite of my heart."

"But you went to the newcomer first, master."

"I was only performing my royal duty. You must try to understand."

"Yes, my master, as long as you love only me."

"You know how much I love you, my queen, my jewel."

"I belong to you, take me in your arms."

"Open your loins for me, sweet love, and receive my royal seed."

I looked at her body, which seemed like a mirror of my own, intimate, yet strangely exciting. Together we rocked, overcome with the sensation of each other. It felt so soft and warm and moist down there. My skin tightened as it rubbed against her pubis. "I can hear your heart beating my love."

"And I can hear yours."

"Now we are one flesh," said Harun-al-Rashid. "Wherever I am, wherever you are, when I call, you must come to me. Nothing can keep us apart. Remember—we are one flesh."

Ursula and Sigrid giggled. I ran back to my own bed and fell instantly and soundly asleep.

Sabina's Sauerkraut

My craving for sauerkraut in the raw goes back to when I was six years old. Propped up in bed (I had the flu), I spent my idle and listless hours watching the cows outside the window. Although they spent the whole day doing the same thing over and over, they never showed the slightest sign of boredom. On the contrary, their satisfaction showed with every mouthful of fresh green grass. I watched them circle clumps of grass with strong, fleshy tongues, then pull up a tasty bunch and munch steadily, without haste. Every so often they looked up dreamily just to chew, totally absorbed, totally content. Knowing my mother would not let me out to graze, I begged her to get me a plate full of raw sauerkraut. I still remember how I masticated the tangy shreds, feeling very much in tune with the cows' intense eating experience.

Unfortunately, I never found a partner willing to share my passion for eating sauerkraut in bed. My husband finds it disgusting, so I do it secretly.

If raw sauerkraut is too kinky for the common tongue, I recommend this cooked version. Although not as elemental, it is equally earthy. Since the ingredients are ordinary kitchen staples, rather than fancy French delicacies, all the credit goes to the imaginative cook, not the gourmet grocer. It satisfies a voracious appetite, which usually follows vigorous exercise and therefore is best served at the conclusion of passionate sex. Only hardy eaters will be able to consume this hearty meal before lovemaking. If, for reasons beyond the control of the cook, the food has to come first, I suggest a brisk walk in the woods as a transition, with an al fresco setting for the post-sauerkraut event.

Drain and rinse one pound of sauerkraut (or a twenty-seven-ounce can) in cold water. Place in a casserole with a large smoked sausage or ham hocks. Add two lean pork chops, and top with a can of diced pineapple, including the juice. Sprinkle with chopped walnuts, coarsely ground pepper, a bay leaf, and a dash of salt. Cover and simmer in a moderate oven for at least two hours. This should leave plenty of time for an unhurried erotic encounter enhanced by the tantalizing aroma from the kitchen. As soon as you are ready to return your attention to cooking—there are no exact time limits—brown four small breakfast sausages in a skillet, drain off the fat, and arrange them on top of the sauerkraut with the other pieces of meat. Serve with fluffy mashed potatoes, garnished with fried onions. (Smoked beef and veal frankfurters can be substituted for a kosher version, and dried fruit with small white beans instead of meat can turn this into a vegetarian meal.)

Recommended for active couples who are seeking a nourishing relationship. The flavor increases with reheating.

II. BODY
LANGUAGE

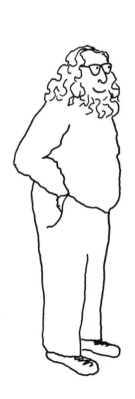

Although our bodies, in art and in life, are capable of inciting passion merely by being stripped of clothing, the excitement of the male body is less in the way it looks *than in the way it* does. *In our stories, the male hero may be paunchy, stoop-shouldered, pale, or thin; his appeal lay elsewhere— in the way he looked at us, the way he moved or spoke, how he explored our body. It is in his body language, we realized, that we revel, and in this sense we found that hesitancy could be as appealing as sureness and playfulness as tantalizing as heavy breathing. When we did focus on his body as object, it was usually a detail—a head of thick, sensuous hair (and gray hair, at that) or a massive hand. Notably, none of our heroes is described as "well endowed."*

In describing our bodies, most of us found it fun to indulge in the narcissism so freely granted (even encouraged) in our own gender. At the same time, we felt comfortable in exposing our imperfections without resorting to Felliniesque ridicule of our shapes and sizes. We particularly delighted in moving from the beheld to the beholder and from the prone to the predatory.

Address to a Penis Owner

We are not anti-penis. In the feminine experience the penis can add the finishing touch to satisfaction, but it is not *sine qua non*. No, indeed. We have been brainwashed into paying more homage than is due this particular attachment of the male anatomy, and far too much has been made of its rise and fall. The fact that we admire a Greek statue no less when the penis has crumbled off should be sufficient proof that male beauty does not depend on this unique feature. Freud, of course, was wrong when he claimed that women suffer from penis envy—it is the men who do. Sadly, a man without a penis is no man at all in our culture, and in male mythology the penis distinguishes a valiant man from a timid one.

We do appreciate a lusty penis when it knows its place. Penis owners should keep in mind that a well-trained penis is a joy to hold and cuddle. If it knows a trick or two, so much the better. A well-behaved penis is indeed woman's best friend, but we object to those mindless penises that indiscriminately push their way in and out of our folds like sewing machines.

We suspect that the penis culture is a male invention from an earlier age when fertility was tantamount to the survival of the race. Understandably, then, the penis is still an important showpiece, and while it also adds much gratification to its owner, it offers comparatively less to the fulfillment of female desires.

If this comes as a shock to you, penis owner, please look at yourself from the female point of view. What is natural to you, who handle your penis many times a day, is quite unnatural to us. To us, the penis is a foreign object. I think that no man knows how alien his rod is to the girl who is confronted with it for the first time, when she is told to stroke it, to lick it, to like it. We know neither the power that comes with owning this tool nor the fear of losing it. Since we don't have anything as obvious and as embarrassingly untrustworthy in our love-making paraphernalia, we share your concern for its ups and downs, so much so that we have obliterated our own needs for gratification. We are not trying to diminish your appendage, but we want to enlarge upon those parts of you that have been unjustly ignored. These are the parts that are essential to our pleasure: your hair, your eyes, your lips, your tongue, your chest, your thighs, your voice, and—most importantly—your hands. It is no accident that our stories have celebrated these greater assets.

DON'T WORRY, HAROLD, SIZE DOESN'T MATTER TO ME.

Hands

The hostess had arranged the dinner table so that "significant others" faced each other, and she had seated us on each side of her at the head of the table. We had settled in to the first course when she asked him the triggering question: "How is your house coming along?"

Whenever he described the house he was building, he became extremely animated. He talked a little faster than usual, his voice rose in pitch and decibels, and his eyes became laser-bright. His "dream house" (as he unabashedly called it) had become a total preoccupation—if he could not be on the site, pacing it out or poring over his plans, the next best thing was to talk about it. To anyone who asked, whether casually or seriously, he turned with eager gratitude, immediately reaching into his shirt pocket for the little notebook he carried, or accepting a proffered scrap of paper, or seizing an unused paper napkin to sketch whatever aspect of the structure intrigued, baffled, or delighted him at the moment. If paper were not available, the open air became his chalkboard as he cupped his hands and fingers around an imaginary piece of chalk and lost himself in passionate drawing—almost but not quite oblivious to the presence of his catalyst, at the moment, our hostess.

From my vantage point across the table from him, I was in a perfect position to watch, yet one more time, his metamorphosis from the man, the dinner guest, my lover, to Master Builder. As always, his face brightened as he began rapidly filling in answers to increasingly sophisticated questions he urgently wanted to answer but she didn't know to ask. Words like "joists," "beams," "lath," "subflooring," and "plenum" darted in and out, and soon became an auditory blur. All I saw were his hands, gesticulating in the air in front of my eyes.

His hands were massive, the fullness at the base of the thumb and the matching column of flesh from wrist to little finger creating a deep sensuous bowl of the inner palm. His fingers were not long and sinewy—the romantic conception of the piano player's fingers—but, rather, thickly gnarled, each one a study in "fingerness." My eyes followed the movement of his hands—coming together, breaking apart, clasping each other momentarily, making sudden twisting motions, freezing for a split second, and then starting their frenzied dance all over again. It was as though I were seeing them for the first time, these hands my body knew so well. I suddenly remembered that they had once fabricated larger-than-life kinetic sculptures which responded to movement and light—intellectually wrought pieces that once out of his hands carried on a life of their own, needing only the passing of a body in front of them to come alive.

As I stared, transfixed, I felt their soft and gentle thickness grip my shoulder, then encircle the back of my taut neck, knowingly and insistently searching me out, discovering each hollow, curve, and subtle shift in skin texture. The warmth of splayed fingers cupped my breasts and trailed downward to my navel, traced the in and out of my hip bone, groin, inner thigh. Beneath his touch, my body became a mound of clay, satin-smooth, moist, elastic. Now yielding, now resisting, twisting, turning, stretching, curling up in feline pleasure, I became the center of an exquisite dance between his hands and my flesh. I shuddered as his hand pressed its heat into my belly and let its fingers slip down quickly into my meadowland, stroking me tenderly, dancing one dance and then another, playing hide-and-seek, disappearing into the cave of me for a split second and then emerging to roll around in the now wet, slippery, pungent grass that sung of spring and wildflowers. From some faraway exotic land I heard the rustle and moan of the wind coming closer and closer and suddenly swelling into a thunderous, piercing cry. Two giant hands reached under me and pulled me upward while a thousand fingers burst into the deep, dark tunnel whose walls endlessly shook and sobbed.

"Darling, you look a bit strange. Are you feeling all right?" The hostess turned to me in concern.

"Yes, I'm fine . . . just fine."

I smiled reassuringly at him and reached across the table to take his hand in mine.

Aerobics

I work out in the back of the studio
knowing that you usually come
late, arriving after the leg lifts and arm rotations,
but always in time for the pelvic thrusts.

You weave your way
past flailing limbs that flash
in metallic tights like thresher blades.

Flat on my back, knees and buttocks
raised, I watch you spread
your legs and join the unison:

> Push, push, squeeeeeeeeze,
> push, push, squeeeeeeeeze,
> 1, 2, 3. 1, 2, 3.
> Now one leg up:
> flex and point, flex and point.
> One more set,
> come on now.
> Don't stop.
> Pelvic tuck.
> Add the head.
> Lift and reach, lift and reach.
> For God's sake, BREATHE!

You are framed between my thighs
and with each head lift, from where I lie,
I can see you strain, eyes shut
tighter than fists,
press, release, press, release,
again and again and again.
With each exhalation
your head alights atop your pubis
like some Aztec god
giving birth to itself.

Da Capo

It has always been his hair, from the beginning, from the first day we met. That day I stared and stared at his hair, which was an exuberance of close-cropped, metal-colored curls, smarting and resentful from the barber's rigorous corrections. His hair was what made him "distinguished looking," but that first day, at the beginning, it was a magnesium flash that shocked me and violated my safety: it made me see myself. I thought I saw my own face ricochet off that gasp of reflected light—lucent, perturbed, vigilant, sly. His name was a label pinned to his lapel. I understood that I would be working for him.

I barely knew him when I started watching my fantasies. These had to do with my hands, which would float to his temples and come to rest, the lacquered fingertips quivering, somnolent as lepidopteral specimens transfixed on a collector's tray. And then, their printless, palpitant, indefatigable caresses, across and through and around the spangled silver wire that shone around his ears and strayed toward the collar of his starched clinical coat.

As we grew less shy with each other, working late on an agenda or collaborating on a report, I found myself becoming more obsessed. The determined boundaries between fantasy and fact began to sag. I noticed that my attempts at disciplining my hand were growing more lax, my movements more languid, more fluent in his company. The phantasmagoria of my dreams, those luxuriant plant forms of milkweed, flax, and blowing prairie grasses, began to assume the rigid boundaries of probable fulfillment. I saw that our shadows flowed ominously together when we met to work; entwining, rending, flooding back into merged stains upon the walls and ceiling even as we sat demurely apart, our bodies serenely isolated from each other's touch. An embrace was thickening the air between us. After five months of collaboration we each knew enough about the other's body signals to wonder who, finally, would make the choice to shed the heavy mantling of reserve lying along our limbs like a refugee's blanket.

One afternoon, standing behind him at his desk while he frowned at the typescript of some minutes I had drafted for him, I made the choice. He leaned forward across his desk to stub out his cigarette in the overflowing ashtray. As he straightened, marking a note in the margin and grunting approval, I moved closer and, stretching out a hand that felt flayed, gently passed the palm across the top of his head. The steely argent of his hair flattened and sprang back like the blazon on a shield. My first sensation was one of complete surprise. I had been expecting tin, sharp, resistant; instead, I found silk. My other hand flew down to join the first for a second opinion. I joined them on top of his head and drew in my breath. I wondered how I would explain my behavior.

With my hands resting on the crown of his head I stared thoughtfully at the enormity of my boldness. What if I were wrong? "You have a cinder on your head," I could say, or, "Just hold still a moment while I remove this lint from your hair." And I could brush, vigorously, with both hands. The words were stillborn on an exhalation. They had no reason for being. I could not pull my hands away. My skin, I found, was subservient to his hair as if it were wet and in contact with live, naked wires. I submitted, then, and let my hands weigh upon his crown.

Dreamily, I began to stroke his brow and temples with my fingertips, the back of my hand, the inside of my wrist. My skin began to tug against my flesh, against my bones. I wanted to feel his hair against all the unexpected surfaces of my skin, against my ankles, under my arms, across my spine where it flares at the base, beneath my chin, around my ears, the nape of my neck. I felt I might weep with temper.

He was so still, so petrified in the amber wash of my obsession that I wondered if time had telescoped, fossilizing us both in the fire and ice of eons precipitated by the force of my agitation and my desire. He was as still and as silent as a mollusk on wet sand, and I thought my breath would stop. Then, in wordless response to the minutest hesitation in my caress, his hands crept around behind his chair and held my legs. I felt my body begin to droop with languor, and I brought one hand down to his shoulder, drawing it softly up the side of his neck and across his chin, which was abrasive from the lateness of the hour. His eyes were closed, and I saw the dark fan of his eyelashes resting on a glint of tears. I brought my cheek down to his marvelous contradictory hair and gently started pulling his head back against my breast. Still he did not open his eyes, and I stared at his face, wondering if my heart would burst my body.

I brought my lips to his brow, to the place between his eyes where they say there is a third eye, the eye of all knowledge. I parted my lips and let the tip of my tongue slide across his eyelids. He jerked back his head and our mouths fell together with an exhalation that rose up from the deepest part of our being, full fathoms five, and still I could not separate my hand from his hair. My fingers writhed and swam like eels trapped in a seine net. I could move among the meshes of his hair but not away. Above us the bars of fluorescent light that lit his office flickered blue as ice.

His face, when I lifted my head to gaze at him, was ashen. His eyes, open now, were like brown, washed pebbles. He watched me with bright hunger and no small distrust. I pressed my face to his hair, nuzzling the silver phosphorescence, and my hands moved down to rest on the lapels of his name-tagged coat. But then my nerves began an agonized appeal that, could it have been heard, would have been a whimper. I had to hold his head, had to feel the live velours of his cropped mane beneath my hands.

And so we remained, beneath the frostlight of the flickering lamp, entwined in that sculptured space while the evening fog lapped the mirrored blackness of the window, speechless, remote. The glittering silence of inanimate objects—the sink and the microscope, the telephone and silver-framed family on his desk—filled the room and illuminated our joined figures at its center as if we, too, were fixtures. Our kisses had pierced the quilted, sterile air like splinters from a smashed bottle of ammonia, and there was no withdrawing.

Later that evening we went to dinner; then we went to bed. We became lovers: luxuriant, inflamed, experimental, preoccupied with the minutiae of voluptuous exchange. Later still we inhabited the same house, embarked upon the manipulation of money and domestic detail. We talked and laughed, wept and lied, fought and felt shame, and made up and always made love. And it's still the same. When I divine his desire, now, after so many years, when he eyes me in a certain way— across the kitchen, emerging from the shower, feeding the cat, on the beach, at the theater—and I move toward him through the folded air, it's still the same. At the moment of contact my hands fly up to his hair, which is white now after all these years. I hold his head in my hands and stroke his hair. I know discovery and reward. The night recedes, my soul escapes, and my body knows good.

Moon Bosoms

How much I dislike hospital banquets, I realize, as I settle into the chair dear Sidney holds out for me. In recent years I have been avoiding these events as more and more staff wives are becoming doctors themselves. Strangely enough, I miss the old days when wives had the freedom of outcasts and clustered together to laugh over common woes. Now, with so many earnest lives focused on medicine, it is almost impossible to escape the medical patter.

The table looks as neat as a hospital bed and is draped with as much linen. I have to lift the tablecloth to make room for my knees, and the large white napkin feels as heavy as a folded sheet on my lap. Gleaming rows of cutlery foretell a long and ponderous meal.

The group at our table look younger and more ostentatiously coifed than ever before. A frizzy permanent obscures the male Asian intern at my left. Two seats beyond I discern that my husband's old rival, now chief of medicine, has sprouted a crown of hair transplants that look more stubborn and painful than thorns. Thank God, Sidney is content to be bald with dignity and resignation!

The spangled ochre jacket of an approaching waiter catches my eye. Carefully lowering a tray of steaming soup bowls to a nearby serving station, he begins serving the guests across the table. I peer anxiously over the chrysanthemum centerpiece, hoping the soup will be madrilene or, better yet, mock turtle. The woman opposite me is being served, and I strain to get a better look at the shimmering golden liquid. Before I can determine what it is, the woman dips the broad base of her spoon into the soup and drops it with a resounding splash.

It happens so quickly and unexpectedly that the woman springs back in her chair with a quick gasp. Her hands rush to her breasts that rise majestically from the pectoral arch to summits barely concealed by folds of blue chiffon. The sight fills me with awe. Each globe nestles blissfully beside its twin, compressed into a deep cleavage that I have always wanted. How warm and reassuring it must be to have them so close together! I try to imagine how their weight and fullness would feel if they were mine. How gently they would jostle each time I moved. They would absorb embraces differently from anything I have known. I wanted to reach out and touch each smooth, peach-soft creamy moon. How totally unlike my own small sinewy body.

The bearer of the bosoms is taking her napkin in her right hand and, with infinite care, slips her left hand under a blue-chiffoned breast and gently cradles it. With the napkin wound around her forefinger, she dabs tenderly at the bulging sphere. I stare transfixed. Has the perfect skin been scalded? My view is obstructed by the hand that wipes and dabs with deliberate and unhurried care.

At last, the hands settle in the woman's lap. The pale alabaster moons glow luminescent. I lean closer to inspect the damage to the left breast, which seems to be of most concern to its keeper. I looks just as perfect as the right one; in fact, I have never seen a more symmetrical pair. Miracles like that, I know, seldom occur in nature.

Sidney, my devoted husband, sitting beside me, has obviously been as spellbound as I by the silent drama that has just unfolded. His years of medical experience tell him that those exquisite breasts probably belong to a nullipara. Their nipples will be pale and pink and the skin light enough to reveal a filigree of veins beneath. During pregnancy these breasts will swell and harden painfully and may be plagued by cracked nipples, engorgement, and possibly infection when nursing commences. The perfect smoothness of the skin may even now conceal lumps of various sizes and textures that will have to be watched and charted in future years.

All this knowledge does not lessen Sidney's desire to lower his face into that delicious cleavage and inhale its natural perfume. He wants to lay his cheek upon those breasts, close his eyes, and float suspended; to lift them from the gown, one by one, and let them hang liberated above the steaming soup; to watch them while she dances, swaying slowly at first, then jiggling as the tempo quickens, until they toss wildly in a tempest of passion. He can feel his hands moving slowly over and around them, marveling at their pliant abundance. He will sink to his knees and gaze up at her twin moons looming overhead and feel protected. The warm underside of each breast will shield his baldness and restore his flagging energy. He wants to lie down and be blatantly seduced.

Sidney glances at me. I stare motionless, tightly coiled, like a cat ready to pounce. My pupils widen, and, had I a tail, it would be twitching. Sidney sees a faint blush rise from my throat to my cheek. He loves the way my color changes when I am aroused. He looks back across the table.

The young woman has a face that is a little too vapid for his liking. She would benefit from some of my intensity. Sidney has always managed in public to quash any sudden lustful feelings, but tonight is different—not because of her but because of my obvious captivation that joins us in sexual conspiracy. I put down my soup spoon and pat his knee. Our eyes meet.

"I caught you," I whisper triumphantly, moving my hand up his thigh and finding his erection.

"You certainly did," he whispers back, "and I caught you!"

We laugh and squeeze hands.

"I was afraid your glasses would fall into your soup," he confides.

"I know," I laugh. "I nearly had to climb the chrysanthemums to get a decent look!"

"For a minute, I thought she was going to feed them some soup. Didn't you?"

I stifle a laugh.

"Of course," he adds loyally, "she won't look as good as you when she's your age."

"Oh, come now. I wish I had them."

"They'll sag pretty soon."

"Fine! I'll take them."

Sidney slips his hand under the folds of tablecloth and fondles my thigh appreciatively. Keeping his hand on my leg, he turns slightly to answer a question about medical politics that issues from his side of the table. As he speaks, I feel his hand begin to creep under my skirt. His long fingers close over the inside smoothness of my thigh and begin tracing small circles. His cool fingertips undulate over my bare skin, and I am thankful that I haven't worn stockings.

At my side of the table the conversation remains on marathon running. I try to look attentive, shifting my gaze from speaker to speaker and laughing on cue with the rest, but all my senses focus on the long fingers that stroke me, slowly advancing from my knee toward my crotch and back again.

The waiter is passing dinner rolls. I draw my legs together abruptly as he approaches, but Sidney does not remove his hand. He refuses the bread with a wave of his other hand and continues to argue the inequities of the present system of medical reimbursement. His little finger wiggles dangerously close to the elastic bindings of my panties and I shift self-consciously in my chair.

Through the remainder of the soup course the pressure of his hand increases. By the time I finish my soup, he is at my panty line, fondling the stray hairs escaping from the lace trim. The waiters are now clearing the soup plates, and I cross my thighs, trapping Sidney's probing hand to keep it still. Not to be thwarted, he keeps his hand locked in place. With infinite patience and unrelenting pressure, he slowly slides his fingers beneath my panty and confidently seeks the secret places he knows so well. My resistance is crumbling.

Waiters start to bring in the entrée, which, to my great alarm, is roast beef. Sidney will need both hands to cut it. I will have to act quickly. Calmly rearranging the large napkin on my lap, I lean closer to the table and begin to butter my dinner roll. As I do, my pelvis rocks forward to increase the pressure of his hand against me. The fingers begin to move more quickly as I bear down more heavily upon them.

The room seems suddenly very hot and full of motion, as though swirling around me. I am a ravenous vortex, recklessly . . .

"Excuse me . . ."

Sidney's fingers freeze. I look up and peer through the chrysanthemums. The bosomed woman is addressing me!

"Excuse me," she repeats, "but would you please pass the butter?"

Backstroke

It was a sultry day. There was a liquid quality to the air that clung suggestively to my skin, and whatever birds had the strength to chirp did so with a throatiness that reminded me they were creatures after all and knew the joys of mating.

It was with these thoughts, barely formed and a little mad, that I had awakened and kicked off the covers—except for the sheet, which I grabbed in my fists and shook up and down so that its white, billowing waves would send cooling jets of air to my sticky flesh. I knew it was no use to shower; clearly, I would be showering all day if this heat kept up. From the closet I pulled out the sheer, gauzelike cotton tunic with its deep V neck and voluminous, pleated folds. I lifted it over my head and let the soft fabric cascade silently over my bare body. It fell to the top of my thighs, just covering the mound of pubic hair that formed a puffy shadow beneath its ivory-colored sheerness. I stood there, not moving, aware of how strangely sensual was the soft filmy fabric that whispered against my hot skin.

I moved to the mirror to see whether the thickness of its folds was enough to obscure the two dots of pink that would otherwise force their way through the flimsiness of the material enveloping me and tell the world I was braless. I twisted and turned, watching myself as if from others' eyes. Would they see? How much would they see? Could I "get away with it"? (Unlike my friends, I had never felt tyrannized by that simple strip of cloth women had flung aside as if it were a chastity belt fabricated by a jealous king protecting his "property" against enemy invasion. In this competitive and breast-obsessed society we shared, my *portobusto* was my friend, magically transforming me from small, and shyly so, to acceptably differentiated from the kings. To be liberated from this precious undergarment was to have my magic carpet stolen from me.)

Still before the mirror, I waved my arms around wildly and bent over to peer down my unfettered cleavage, again scrutinizing myself from the perspective of others. The delicate texture of the material played against my skin, teased my nipples, caressed my back. I was giddy with the myriad and discrete sensations I was feeling. Light breezes of hot air surprised my arms and flew against my armpits, awakening my flesh in fragments. No longer was my torso an undifferentiated mass of tissue, muscle, and bone. The absence of my familiar undergarments was palpable. Incongruously, Robert Frost's criticism of free verse, as being like playing tennis with the net down, popped into my head.

I slipped into a pair of soft, cotton pantaloons, tucking the folds of the blouse inside the elasticized waistband. The contrast of bound and free excited me. The snugness of the band around my waist heightened the sensations of airiness encircling my upper body, and the now double-layer of fabric below clung to my moistened skin like a warm girdle of loving hands.

Throughout the morning, I walked around the house reveling in my discovered body just as the avant-garde artist delights in the "found object." At the same time, I waited for the teasing sensations to give way to the ordinariness of the body I knew as mine. Instead, I became more and more restive, more and more tantalized—it was as if I was being held in a state of excitation that would not let go. The fantasy of two massive hands pressing gently against my back quivered in me like a suppressed scream.

As if in answer to my thoughts, the doorbell rang. He was "just dropping by, hoping you'd be home." He moved to embrace me (we were still new enough to each other for that), and I threw myself into his arms with a wantonness he had never seen in me. I kissed him passionately and felt his eager response pressing hard against me. He pulled the flimsy fabric of my blouse out from under its entrapping belt and moved his hands up and across the imaginary pathway—illicit, vulnerable, and acutely conscious of where the strap was supposed to be. I sensed the startle in his hands as he hesitated a second, then quickly slid them down again as if to affirm that the border patrol forbidding entry into erogenous zones was no longer there. With the realization, his hands sped like lightning to my breasts, cupping them gently in his hands and making bumpy fistlike protrusions under the cotton fabric that hung loosely between us. The more ardently he fondled my breasts, the more I yearned to feel his warm and powerful hands on my back, sliding up and down my alert and now abandoned flesh. I reached under the teasing fabric to find his eager hands, and, ever so gently, moved them from my breasts to my back. He looked at me, perplexed. I had no answer for him—only my silent ecstasy as his hands, mindless and warm, slowly restored my body to its rightful owner.

Snake Dance

Although it was near midnight, the heat of the day still rose from the parched desert floor and warmed the blanket beneath us like an electric pad. In the absence of a moon, the desert glowed with starlight. The sight of so much unfathomable space made me feel weightless, and I was certain I would have tumbled into that cold, black void if it had not been for the closeness of Dave and Garth sleeping on either side of me.

Our long drive had left me hyperalert. I listened tensely, expecting any moment to hear the high whine of a mosquito, and immediately my exposed skin began to itch. Beetles most certainly were crawling beneath the blanket searching for crumbs while bats probably fluttered and swooped low overhead. Crickets were singing, and somewhere quite close I heard tiny feet scamper. A shiver ran across me, and I turned toward Garth's reassuring bulk. It lay slack and still, the rhythm of his breathing slow and regular.

Dave lay against my back, and I could feel him start to turn stealthily toward me. He paused, motionless and taut, and lay in wait for silent minutes. Then, very quietly, his legs and arms enfolded my curled, fetal form, and his lean body pressed close. We fit together like two stacked chairs. Furtively, his hands inched under my blouse and massaged my back with soft, circular strokes. I was almost ready to be lulled to sleep like that when his hands slipped around my sides and cupped each breast. The wakened part of me shuddered with pleasure, and I straightened. With his hands on my breasts, Dave rolled me over on top of him. On my back with the Milky Way above and Dave's rigid body below, I took each of his hands in mine and guided them over my hips and belly.

Garth was stirring now, attracted by the sensuous movement. He awakened with mindless readiness and turned toward us. Fingers and tongues explored the terrain of my torso and traveled its mounts and open plains, its canyons and crevices. Limbs slid over limbs like a slithering tangle of hungry boas and shed their garments like discarded snakeskins. Shutting my eyes, I imagined serpents braiding and coiling themselves into a moving maze of gleaming scales. The skein of muscled strands tied knots to no avail and tunneled in and out upon themselves. I felt myself rise and swell to their touch. Waterfalls thundered in my ears. Arctic lights swirled behind closed lids. Earthquakes shook my thrusting pelvis, and the deepest quicksand churned in my tissued core. The unguided head of a penis butted its way toward my safe, wet enclosure, while another groped blindly along my thigh. Serpentine limbs flexed with a sense of destiny now and hastened toward conclusion. The multitude of predators and prey clasped each other in a paralyzing grip and, with a series of great spasmodic gulps, released. I opened my eyes and saw the entire galaxy swirling.

The Look

The look was brief
a whisper of a glance
a breath that rustled ferns.
A look so small it
was not recorded
on galactic time.
Still in that silent glance
hardly inhabited by
a whirling electron,
I felt the crystal pinwheels
of your energy,
a bomb exploding
fragments of your space
to mine.

Eyes

She looked up and her eyes met his. They were alone in a corner, so no one was near enough to hear her. She swallowed, dropped her shoulders, and lowered her gaze for a second. Then she looked at him squarely and said: "Let's leave this boring party." His eyes opened wide. "What did you say?"

"I said, let's leave this boring, boring party!"

"What do you have in mind?" his eyes glinted back at her, his head tilted naughtily.

"I know a secret place, and there are things I'm dying to do . . . with you." A tiny blush crept up her neck, and she squirmed just a little on her chair.

His mouth opened a bit as she spoke. "Tell me, what things?" His eyes probed hers for answers.

She looked at the place where his shirt came to a V. Dark tendrils played there. Her nostrils flared, and she breathed a little faster.

"I want to touch your chest." Her eyes fixed there. She had never seen such a hairy body—lovely black curls flecked with gray, sparkling, twisting. She could almost feel the resilience of those curls pressed against her breast and belly. "And I want to lie down next to you."

"Will you let me undress you?" he asked, without a bit of shyness. "I've got a giant hard-on. When can we go?"

"First, tell me what you want to do with me," she smiled, teasing a little now.

"My god, I want to see you naked sitting on my cock, moving up and down and sideways with your hair down around your shoulders."

"Jesus, no build-up?"

He relaxed a little. "The build-up will have to wait for the second fuck."

"Yes . . . ?"

"I'll start by oiling you up and giving you a long massage—you'll tell me where you like it, and I'll stroke and lick those places—for as long as you want. I'll roll you over on your stomach and slip into you from behind. Just when you're . . ."

The hostess walked toward them smiling. "You two must meet one another. You can't just sit here any longer not speaking—Arn, Sandy."

Sandy cleared her throat and spoke her first words to Arn: "Has anyone ever told you what marvelously expressive eyes you have?"

Hot Pursuit

Someone was following her. Now she was certain. It was very early to be out. There was no traffic to blunt her perception, no bystanders to help her either.

The footfalls, a faint pulse at first, could now be heard distinctly: soft, steady slaps upon the pavement. They didn't land with the ominous thud of boots or with the sinister click of pointed shoes with silver heel taps. The light, clean beat behind her announced a less threatening sort—someone young and quick in soft-soled shoes.

Five yards beyond, there was a side street. She decided to turn right onto it to allay her suspicion. She turned the corner, determined not to break her stride, and counted off the quiet seconds. At the fourteenth she heard the steps again. She listened for them to cross the street and to fade in the direction she had been going.

They didn't. They had turned the corner onto the narrow street. The deliberate, regular gait sounded louder now, almost matching hers, but heavier. Short exhalations, then a cough, punctuated the air. It was a man.

The next intersection loomed a half-block ahead. She would not glance back. Confidence. Stay calm. Keep moving.

The patter of their footsteps became sloppy, overlapping. They were no longer in synch. His footsteps landed faster, nearer. His breath was deep and regular, undeniable—a percussive breath that radiated desire, primitive and hot, leaving frosty puffs in the crisp morning air. The closeness of his respiration propelled her. Her ears and neck felt suddenly flushed, and she quickened her pace.

Her hair bounced loose and free as if reaching out tentacles to explore her pursuer. Her legs felt long and strong. She wanted to go on like this for miles, bounding lithe and muscled through empty city streets like a modern Atalanta with Hippomenes panting at her heels. Her pulse beat to the rhythm of his breath.

Suddenly he sprinted forward. Her thrill rose in her throat as he brushed past her left elbow and whispered a breathless "Nice goin'."

She never broke her stride and never took her eyes off his firm buttocks flashing in flimsy white running shorts until he rounded the corner and vanished.

Vegetable Love

From the beginning they had described their relationship as a kind of miracle, for so it seemed in the easy way they had moved together right from the first. It was as though they had leaped over that period of adjustment all couples are supposed to go through: when he discovers that she hangs wet underwear in the bathroom and she discovers that he wears the same socks three days in a row. Whenever they talked about the miraculousness of their being together, they laughed about it furtively, like children who had "got away with" something. But they also knew that miracles had a voracious appetite, demanding constant feedings of magic.

He would be home soon. It was her night to "manage" the meal, his to be "in service"—a formula they had agreed on when they first moved in together two years ago. They usually made a game of it, easily dropping the mother-to-son or master-cook-to-helper roles that invaded other liberated kitchens, mostly because neither knew how to cook with any finesse. She had already decided to have the broiled herb chicken again— the one fail-safe recipe she had learned from her last lover.

She moved quickly to the refrigerator and took out the chicken breasts. She laid them side by side in a pyrex baking dish, doused them with oil, and, just as David used to do, randomly opened one herb jar after another, crumbling blossoms and stems between her thumb and forefinger and letting them fall over each breast in a warm green herbal blanket that darkened the glistening oil. (If David had been making informed selections, it never showed: "Hmmm, this smells good," he would say with his nose in the jar, and it then joined the others.) She left the chicken to soak up the oil and herbs, took the asparagus and cherry tomatoes from the crisper, and placed the asparagus on one side of the double sink and the cherry tomatoes on the other.

"What now?" she said to herself as she stood in the middle of the room, looking around and making mental notes of how their meal preparation should go. They could do the vegetables together while the chicken was broiling, and then set the table. On a sudden inspiration, she pulled out an unopened box of twelve slender candles designed to fit the wrought-iron circular candle holder she used as a centerpiece on special occasions. She carefully fit each tapered candle into its ball-like enclosure, and then set the holder on the window sill over the sink where they would be standing. She lit each candle and stood back to survey the effect. They had the festive look she wanted, and there was just enough daylight left for them to see what they were doing.

As she gathered together the various things they would need— colander, salt, pepper, paper towels, cooking pot for the asparagus, serving dishes—she heard his key in the lock. She turned the oven dial to *Broil* and went to meet him in the hallway, as if he were the first invited guest to a dinner party.

He moved toward her, his arms open wide, and looked intently into her face. He slipped his hands under her loose blouse and pulled her close. She rubbed her cheek against his, kissed his ear lightly, and then pulled away. Someone watching would have said they had been together two weeks instead of two years.

"Come on," she said. "Hungry?"

She drew him into the kitchen and over to the sink where the candles twinkled down on the vegetable display. He smiled and squeezed her hand.

"Great. I love it. What's my job?" he said. Whatever scenario she created, he always joined in with gusto.

"Well, first the chicken goes in the broiler, and then we get to play vegetables by candlelight. Okay?"

He had the chicken into the broiler in an instant and was back at her side.

"You take the tomatoes," she said, "I'll do the asparagus."

46

She picked up an asparagus spear and held it under water, flicking her finger lightly over its fragile tip. She watched him pick up the first tomato, pluck out the tiny stem embedded in its navel, and roll it around in his hand under the cold water. On impulse, she took it from him and placed it in his surprised mouth where he held it like a round red kiss he was unwilling to release. The saltshaker was on his side of the sink; she circled her arms around him, pressing her breast against his arm as she reached for it. He watched now as she sprinkled salt in her hand and licked it up with the tip of her tongue. She held out her salt-flecked tongue to him and he moved his mouth toward hers, gently pushing the tomato from his lips to hers. She bit into it gently and offered him the remaining bulge of its red flesh. They chewed solemnly and in unison while their eyes laughed silently at each other. Again, he pressed his half-open mouth to hers; she let her tongue play around the soft inner flesh of his lips until his eyes became cyclopean. She drew back and smiled mischievously. He placed his still damp hands on her buttocks and pulled her body tightly to his. She felt his warm hardness against her pubic bone.

"It's time to do something with the asparagus," she whispered.

"Yeees," he said, in that slow, teasing way he had. "Shall we?" His meaning was clear.

"Right *now?*" she asked.

In answer, he started to take off her clothes and, in a scramble, they undressed each other. In what felt like one continuous motion, he pulled her over to the straight-back chair, sat down, and lowered her body onto his. When she felt him just barely inside her, she held her body taut and poised. He clutched her hips and began to move her pelvis in slow circles around him. He burrowed his head between her breasts, then let his mouth linger on one nipple, pulling in and releasing it as she sucked in and released the silken, round tomato perched on his sturdy stalk. She took his face in her hands and stared openly and fixedly at the tangle of expressions that played around his mouth, his jaw, his eyes, knowing that her own face mirrored them back to him. Pulling his head closer to her body, she buried her hands in his hair.

The ring of the telephone suddenly burst its presence into the room and, as if wired to it in some way, he pulled her body down hard and fast on his. They clung to each other through the violent spasms that shook through them. Her body finally collapsed, her head dropping into the hollow of his neck. He stroked her hair gently and mumbled softly in her ear as the phone rang relentlessly, the chicken sputtered, and the candles bravely held on to their last flickering light.

Tantric Sex

Directions for Tantric sex:

1. Man and woman sit nude on the floor, facing each other. The woman moves as close to the man as possible and puts her legs over the man's legs and around his body. The man circles her body with his legs. The arms are relaxed on the partners' hips. Both take several deep breaths, rest their gaze on the left eye of the other and meditate together, eyes open for 5 to 10 minutes.

2. The partners move closer, and the woman puts her mouth near the man's left ear. Feeling the movement of his breath, she replicates the rhythm in his ear, breathing his breath. (Do this meditation for 5 minutes.) They move their heads to the other side and the man replicates the rhythm of the woman's breath. (Do for 5 minutes.) They shift heads again. Starting with their individual rhythms, the partners slowly arrive at a common rhythm, "breathing the one breath." (Continue this meditation for as long as is enjoyable.)

3. After gentle loveplay, the woman introduces the erect penis into her well-lubricated vagina, in the same posture described in exercises 1 and 2. Through periodic contractions of her vaginal muscles and occasional slight movements by the man, both partners attempt to keep the penis erect without thrusting. Both breathe deeply and are sensitive to the flow of energy between them. *

*Reprinted with permission of Stella Resnick, Ph.D., from her article, "The Erotic Lifestyle: Being Turned On," published in *New Age*, August 1978.

I felt very lusty and the children were all gone. It was late in the afternoon. I told him I wanted to try Tantric sex.

"What's that?"

"It's when you don't move, and I'm not sure if you're supposed to have an orgasm."

So we got completely undressed, sat down on the floor, and began.

Step number one was very strange for me. The position was easy enough to assume, but "resting my gaze on the left eye of the other and meditating, eyes open, for 5 to 10 minutes" made me very uncomfortable. It was as though that eye had been disembodied and was free-floating. It could as easily have been a stranger or a statue I was gazing at. I always seek eye contact with people to whom I'm speaking, but this was different, bizarre. Maybe I could learn to like it.

Step number two started off very badly. While replicating the rhythm of his breath in his ear, my stomach kept sending little gurgles upward to my throat—it was very distracting and very unerotic. I really tried hard not to laugh. We shifted right away to "breathing the one breath." For me this was an extremely profound experience.

The sensation of being nude, sitting about as close together as two people can, arms around one another, in daylight, was novel and very exciting. We breathed together like this for a long time. I think I felt a little dizzy. It transcended any verbal communication we have ever had. It was probably the closest I have ever come to having a spiritual experience. I did feel our spirits merging together in a way that was extremely different from joining together sexually.

Then, as though in a dream, and in slowest motion, the spiritual closeness dissolved and merged into a physical union as body parts slipped together gently, quietly, and almost motionless. The feeling of transcendence remained with me. I was being taken out of my body. But the pulsing and throbbing was a reminder of our two very real bodies joined together, almost still, but with a powerful energy flowing between us. The heat and the accelerated throbbing in my groin reduced me once again (or should I say expanded me once again!) into a purely physical being. I resisted the overwhelming desire to move—to grind—but the throbbings were growing into contractions now, which were out of my control. The contractions continued to grow and swell until they were so mighty they broke loose. My body stiffened and rocked back and forth for several long seconds, then sighed and slumped, exhausted.

I returned rather quickly to the quiet house and the afternoon.

Farewell, Fanny

I can hear your plea
for a slimmer me,
but I like my ass
although it's crass.
My powerful seat
may be fashion's defeat,
but in blaming my bottom
you must have forgotten
my lava fountain
inside that mountain,
my cradle of fire
to rock your desire.

I'm not blind
to your taboos—
feel free to choose
another kind
and leave my own
behind.

Rose's Spring Lamb

There are "leg men," and there are "leg women." As a "leg woman" nothing catches my eye faster than a well-turned leg of young spring lamb, one that tapers leanly toward the shank but bulges firmly in the thigh.

Once I am smitten by such a leg, I eye my friend, the butcher. He winks back in collusion, like Cupid arranging the perfect match, and cheerfully bones it for me. I rush home to massage it with a savory blend of curry and a clove or two of garlic. After allowing the spices to penetrate the lamb at room temperature for several hours, I barbecue it over glowing coals flecked with ash. The cooking time varies depending on the thickness of the meat and the heat of the fire, but thirty-five to forty-five minutes is usually enough. Touch it often as it cooks. It should feel firm and springy if you want it pale pink and juicy inside.

Sometimes if the leg is very large, I will cut the tougher half into cubes for shish kebabs. Let the cubes soak for several hours or a day in a piquant marinade. For the marinade, blend two teaspoons of Dijon mustard together with a crushed clove of young garlic, a generous pinch of oregano and basil, a bay leaf, some chopped parsley, freshly ground black pepper, and a small chopped onion. Then, as if you were making a vinaigrette, whip in a quarter cup of red wine vinegar or sherry and three-quarters of a cup of purest virgin olive oil. This marinade will permeate the lamb and soften the toughest fibers.

When you are ready to barbecue, thread the lamb chunks onto skewers along with a riot of red and green peppers, button mushrooms, cherry tomatoes, zucchini, bacon, or whatever you choose. Cook close to hot coals for twenty to twenty-five minutes, basting frequently with the remaining marinade.

III. LONGING FOR
A STRANGER

Our "stranger" stories came relatively early in the history of the Kensington Ladies' Erotica Society. Paradoxically, whatever danger they pose in real life, strangers, in fiction at least, served as people we could turn to safely, indulging our fantasies and longings without exposing our private lives. For some of us, the longings took an exotic turn, but for others, the escapade was on familiar turf. Perhaps what we did reveal was a restiveness with our everyday world—a yearning to have it come alive in a way it never could in "real life." In committing our "strange loves" to paper, we discovered that we had created a host of warm bodies whose presence is now very real.

My Gardener

I answered his ad in September's *Tribune,* and he came in a battered Volkswagen with Rolf, a gentle collie-shepherd mix, who greeted me like a long-lost friend. Needing no better recommendation, I immediately asked him to walk with me through the remains of a garden still clinging to life despite a two-year drought. He was full of concern and empathy for the quiet struggle taking place before him. He stood very close as we stooped over the wilted beds and droopy rhododendrons and crossed the long-dead lawn. We studied the singed remains of a great, old birch that had already dropped its leaves a month before. He rapped the trunk with his knuckles—hard, dull thumps—and then leaned over to tear some turf from around the base. I could see the rippling flexion of his back muscles through the thin, faded fabric of his plaid workshirt.

"We should keep this cleared," he said, "and then try some deep watering. I think it can be saved."

I showed him down some flagstone steps to a lower terrace enclosed by a towering hedge of dying privet.

"Have you ever thought of replacing that?" he asked.

"Yes, if only I could budge them."

He strode over and with a great heave ripped one out.

"That's magnificent," I cried. The gap revealed a shimmering view of the bay and city beyond. The late afternoon sun blazed from across the Golden Gate directly into our eyes. The shock of the glare was as startling as the intent gaze of his blue eyes, so pale that they generated a light of their own. He stood at least a head taller than me, and as he smiled down, I felt embraced. With a focus so intensely intimate, surely the plants would be healed! I hired him.

Every week he comes. Sometimes when I am home, we work side by side in the dirt. He moves with a grace and gentleness that brings the most reluctant seedlings to life. His strong forearms are tanned and covered with sun-bleached hairs. Being close to him in the sunshine fills me with a contentment so complete that when I realize it, I become self-conscious and jump up to offer him iced tea.

If I remain indoors, he often rings the doorbell, sometimes with a question about what to do next. Other times he calls me out of the house in great excitement to show me a remarkable discovery. Just last week he led me through some brambles to a clearing where he had uncovered a hydrangea smothering a sword fern. I watched as he knelt and clipped back more of the lush hydrangea and exposed the long, shiny, serrated leaves of the fern. Then he leaned back, sitting on his heels, and said, "I like this. It pleases me. It really pleases me." It was all I could do to keep from lowering my arms around his neck and burying my face in his soft tousled curls.

Instead I returned to the house. It is my retreat and safety—clearly off-limits to him. My life here is devoted to my husband and children. Everything is as it should be. He is careful never to enter except, perhaps, to use the basement bathroom.

Usually he comes to tell me when he's leaving and what he plans to do next time. We confer long and seriously on the drafty front step. Our talk stays scrupulously focused on gardening—on color, arrangement, and natural ways to combat pests. We are both averse to using sprays and poisons, though I do occasionally resort to using snail bait. He is certain that rain is imminent and wants to get the clearing and fall planting finished as soon as possible. He lingers politely on the step like a courting knight, afraid to take too great a liberty yet reluctant to leave without some small encouragement.

I stand riveted in the doorway relishing his wholehearted attention. He stands so near that I can feel the warmth radiating from his body and can detect the sweet fragrance of castile soap. The smoothness of his shave is remarkable, even in the late afternoon. He must use a straight razor, and I imagine him going through his meticulous routine with the same care that he lavishes on my plants. While we discuss the best ways to cultivate compost, I see him after his shower standing before a mirror wearing nothing but the shaving lather on his face. I imagine his razor scraping wide careful strokes around his soft lips, but I cannot bear to picture the final swaths of the razor's edge over his arched pulsing throat.

As September comes to an end, my gardener's appearances become more and more frequent. I am often surprised to find him at unexpected times—just as I am rushing out to take my youngest to nursery school or as I return from a run, all sweaty and flushed. Often in the late afternoons when I am home between car pooling, he is back, loading his Volkswagen for trips to the dump. His dog waits in the driveway to intercept me and leads me proudly by the wrist to his admiring master like a retriever delivering a prize.

When the clearing and tilling are completed, my gardener asks me to meet him at the local nursery to select fall plants. I agree, and when I arrive at the appointed time, he is already waiting. He beams at me in mock astonishment.

"My God! A skirt!" he exclaims. "I've never seen you in a skirt!"

"Really?" I blush, glad to have worn a new dress and even gladder to be able to walk the gravel path in new wedgy heels without wobbling. I love being *seen* again!

"You know what you need?" he says in a low voice.

"What?" I ask expectantly.

"Lilac."

"Oh, why yes. You're right. We don't have that, do we?" I hope my voice doesn't convey my disappointment.

"It will be magnificent near your roses next spring," he continues and places his hand on my shoulder to gently guide me to the shrubbery section.

We meander up and down the long, moist rows of shrubs. He helps me sidestep puddles, and I feel exquisitely protected. He tells me bits of esoteric information about the plants and how the different varieties adapt to the Bay Area's microclimates. I savor the gentle timbre of his voice.

We arrive at the lilacs.

"These look healthy and pretty well established," he observes. He bends over a five-gallon-sized bush and pokes the earth around its base.

"Here's one that's nice and full," I say as I wander down the row.

He looks at my selection, takes my hand, and guides me back to his. My hand feels small and cold inside his.

"Yes, but it looks a little forced. I like the root system better on this one. That's what we have to consider at this time of year." He holds my hand a little longer, and I happily concede.

With the coming of October, my gardener's prediction comes true: the rains come early. Storm after storm sweeps in from the Pacific. The parched ground soon becomes soggy. Permanent puddles grow into small lakes. Weeds and forget-me-nots sprout lavishly. Ivy threatens to strangle everything, and snails ooze triumphantly over all.

One drenched day I arrive home from a seminar, full of fresh thought and resolve, and find my gardener staking up rhododendrons.

"I just can't work in weather like this," he calls as I emerge from my car. Without a second though I invite him in for coffee. After all, it is safe—my son and a babysitter are upstairs.

We run up the flagstone path to the shelter of the doorway. He unlaces his boots and lays them neatly beside the mat as I unlock the door and lead the way inside. He enters carefully, attentively, noticing everything. He strays into the living room saying that he loves the colors in the bright Moroccan rug. I am about to apologize for the clutter when he says how warm and welcoming he finds our scattered collections of shells, rocks, and other found treasures. He stops in front of an array of Barbie dolls in various stages of garish dress and undress in the middle of the room. A naked Ken and Barbie stand paralyzed in an awkward kiss. Next to them a platinum-haired rival in a tutu lies face down on a hand mirror, and the severed head of a Million Dollar Man stares glassily at the ceiling.

"Egad, what's this?" he asks.

"Just an unfinished game," I explain. "I think one day my daughter and her friends will write their manifesto, and it'll be called *Our Barbies, Ourselves*."

He laughs and follows me into the kitchen—the inner sanctum at last! He perches on a stool at the high cooking counter and watches me make coffee.

"I've never seen you more radiant," he comments.

I tell him about my exciting morning—how I am just beginning to realize there's life after school.

"What do you mean?" he asks, leaning forward on folded arms.

I bring coffee over on a wicker tray and sit across from him. His hair clings in damp ringlets about his face. I inhale the rich mingling aromas of his wet hair and the freshly brewed coffee.

"I stayed a student barnacle too long," I confess. "I clung to institutions. I couldn't bear to graduate so I went on to graduate school and then taught. I kept going from one incubator to another."

"I know what you mean," he nods sympathetically. "I stayed attached too long, too."

"You did? To what?"

"I was in a seminary for eight years."

I am nonplussed. He seems too physical, too much a part of the natural world for that.

"So you see," he continues, shifting slightly on his stool, "I have some catching up to do."

"That's hard," I answer. He suddenly seems so vulnerable and alone that I reach out instinctively and hold his hand.

Just then we hear the sound of footsteps pounding down the stairs. He pulls his hand back abruptly as my child and the babysitter appear.

"I'm hungry," announces my son, surveying the scene with enormous, unfaltering dark eyes. He climbs possessively into my lap. "Isn't it lunch time?"

"Yes, almost. Aren't you going to say hello?"

My child gives an uncompromising nod.

"I have to be leaving now," says the sitter.

"So should I," says my gardener. "I'll be back when the weather clears."

I usher them to the door, pay the sitter, and return to the kitchen. My small guardian stands on the counter and looks down accusingly.

"Why was the gardener here?"

"It's raining, so I asked him in for coffee."

"Why does he look at you that way?"

"What way?"

"Y'know . . . with his eyes."

"You mean he should look at me with his nose?"

"Ohhhh, Mom! Where's lunch anyway?"

Halfway through lunch the phone rings. It is my gardener sounding urgent, saying he needs to talk right away. Is this a good time?

I look at my alert companion watching from across the counter and tell him to call back in an hour.

"Who was that?" asks my son.

"The gardener."

"What does he want?"

"I don't know."

"Why does he have to call back?"

"Maybe he wants to ask for a raise," I blurt out, suddenly appalled by my logic.

I reflect on our morning visit and wonder if I was wrong to have invited him inside. Has our physical attraction grown too huge for him to bear? Perhaps he will have to find other work. What terrible revelation am I about to hear? I glance at the clock and wait.

At two o'clock exactly, the doorbell rings. I am startled because I had expected him to phone. I open the door, and he is perched on his accustomed step huddled in his rain jacket with his arms crossed over his chest. He looks down at his boots and balances carefully on one foot, then the other.

"I have to talk to you . . .," he begins. "This thing's been on my mind a lot lately, and I just don't feel comfortable with it."

"Yes, tell me," I say, bracing myself.

He shakes his tousled hair and sighs. Then, looking sorrowfully into my eyes, he says, "The snail bait . . . I . . . I just can't use it . . . not in such quantity . . . not with your pets and children around. I just can't do it."

"Oh, that's all right," I soothe, hardly believing my ears. "Don't worry. You don't have to kill in my garden."

"Oh, phew," he laughs. "I've been hoping you'd say that."

Smiling at my munificence, I watch him stride down the glistening flagstone path to his Volkswagen. Snails may come and go, but a good gardener is hard to find.

IDEAL LOVER

The Leopard:
A Fairy Tale for Responsible Adults

Doctor Bingham yawned. It was hard to concentrate in this humid, sweetly perfumed climate. The electricity was out again, and without air-conditioning the tropical heat made her fall into dreamy lethargy. The new hotel with only one wing completed in time for the conference already suffered from decay, as if termites were eating away the cheaply constructed walls. The toilets didn't flush, and the refrigerators could not keep their Western diets frozen. Like a python, the rain forest waited only one mile away to swallow up this frail hybrid of a Hilton Hotel and with it the resolutions of this international group of experts. In a few days they would all return to their temperate laboratories and scientific organizations, and the naked walls of this conference room would soon be covered with exotic fungus. Melissa wearily read over her notes. So far she had gone to every lecture. She always went to the lectures. The Global Food Fund relied on Melissa Bingham's reports.

The next speaker was Claudio Torres de Valle y Monteverde. She recognized his handsome face from a *Time* magazine article. His family had done things for the country—on horseback with swords and later with land reforms. Now, the family stripped of political power, Claudio championed the causes of the dispossessed against global greed. Melissa was prepared to distrust his flamboyant optimism about his country's natural resources. Therefore, she did not mind that he delivered his paper in Spanish. Courtesy demanded that she stay in her seat, but she would have given anything to get away.

Then, the totally unexpected happened. As soon as he took charge of the lectern, she was under his spell. Although everyone else wore shirt sleeves and rumpled khakis, he wore an immaculate suit of European cut. He was brazenly at ease in this climate. The gleaming white shirt accentuated the nutmeg luster of his skin, and the open collar revealed a heavy necklace of native onyx. In vain she struggled against his self-possessed charm, his disconcerting grace. His open smile welcomed her, singled her out from all the others as if he wanted her alone to listen, as if only she could understand him. Shifting uncomfortably in her seat, she tried to muster some scientific smugness, but she could not take her eyes from him. He looked at her as if they were alone. What game was he playing? The answer came straight from her groin. She blushed. He was undressing her, appraising her body. How dare he breach her anonymity as a fellow scientist? She was outraged. No she wasn't. She was excited, turned on.

Instead of hiding behind her notes, she decided to teach him a lesson in equality. Ostentatiously, she removed the translation phones from her ears. Boldly, she stared at his broad shoulders and narrow hips, savoring him piece by piece. Did he notice? He noticed. For a moment he seemed distracted—good. She understood enough Spanish to recognize that he was searching for words. She smiled, amused. Clearly he understood that she could play her own game. Unlike the other speakers, including herself, he was not chained to the lectern. He pranced back and forth like an elegant leopard, wanting them all, forcing them to pay attention to him.

Melissa decided to relax and enjoy his performance. She saw a hunter who pursued his prey, devoured it lovingly, tenderly, and in turn wanted to be captured, devoured, and consumed by the huntress. His body was both soft and powerful, and so was his voice. Now and then the meaning of a word would reach her ears, but all she wanted to hear was the voice. Closing her eyes, she saw him nude. Disturbingly seductive, his voice conjured up his lithe body, silken to the touch, vibrant, potentially wild. The language suited his voice—a melodious European Spanish, the heavy vowels of Castile, so smooth without the hissing "s" of Latin America. His language had been polished like driftwood by centuries of formal use, by poetry and courtly love. Like the flutes the natives carved of ebony, it was a well-tuned instrument, which released its secret powers slowly after years of practice. Only a master could play the haunting melodies, blending the sound of human and animal love calls. She wanted to be alone with that voice.

"I want you to cry out to me, to expose your secret life to me. I want your lips on my breast, your breath in my ears, all over me. I want soft consonants to rain over my thighs, full-blooded vowels to penetrate my inmost being. I want to taste your lips like exotic fruit. I want to see your words glisten like drops of crystal, and I want you to put them around my neck, my belly, and my ankles."

When the lecture was over, Melissa filed out of the room after the others, scarcely aware of the faces and remarks of her colleagues. She wanted to bump into him, but he was nowhere to be seen. Without hesitation, she stepped inside the taxi that idled in front of the hotel. The driver said something about a restaurant at the harbor where everyone from the conference was going. She nodded. She knew he was taking her to her leopard.

The drive was beautiful along a coastal route that dipped into coconut groves and climbed over rocky cliffs. When the car stopped at a vine-covered terrace, nestled into the hillside high above the ocean, she did not flinch when she heard the extravagant sum of money that the driver demanded for the ride. Her foundation obviously knew what they were doing when they allotted a generous amount for travel expenses. But they had refused to pay for a child's ticket; how full of wisdom was the male working world to free her for this adventure. She smiled when she paid and added a large tip. "Did she want him to wait?" asked the driver. No, she did not care to think about going back—ever.

As if gliding on tracks, she moved among the tables crowded with people. She had seen him right away. He sat alone. Miraculously, an empty chair waited across from him.

"Excuse me," she said, "this seems to be the only seat available. Is it taken?" He gestured toward it invitingly. "It is yours, Doctor Bingham."

"I see, here we all are again. I thought I was getting away from the conference." Melissa blushed, removing her name tag.

"The taxis always take a longer route. Our friends came by charter bus. This is the only restaurant within miles." He played the host; only a faint smile hinted at their conspiracy. She had counted on finding him alone.

"I suppose we are all eating the same thing," she said crossly.

"I recommend the scampi; you won't find better ones anywhere." Then he purred: "I have been wanting to tell you how much I appreciate your coming. You are one of the few Americans who understand my views. I read your article in *World Nutrition*. You know our problem here. I can show you what really goes on with American money. I wanted very much to talk to you, but—well, I expected somebody—I thought you were—I mean, I had no idea, that you were so attractive." Again she blushed, proud to be recognized, but she was running away from being Dr. Bingham. If she took back her professional identity the magic would be gone forever. She looked at this polite gentleman who spoke English fluently. Where was the leopard? "I hope, I have not offended you?" She remained silent while the waiter stripped the gigantic prawns from the skewers. Obviously he had waited for her to order his meal. She decided to risk all.

"I find you very attractive too." She trembled inside as she forced herself to look at him. Then she boldly raised her glass.

"Salud," answered the leopard. She watched him pull off the pink shell tenderly and with mouth-watering anticipation. Deftly he lifted the plump creature to his lips holding it by its tail.

"Smell it first," he ordered. She tried to follow his example but shrank at first from snapping off the head with its delicate feelers. She was not used to smelling her food like that but did as she was told before biting into the succulent flesh. It was firm, but not tough—freshly caught, no doubt. The taste of garlic and lemon was enticing, but some other exotic flavor had been added. She asked him what it was. He explained that the special wood in the broiler made the difference. "They cure the wood; that is the secret."

"Ah, yes," she nodded, picking up another tail and licking it gingerly with her tongue, appreciating the crisply stretched inner skin. To savor the flavor fully, she chewed slowly, as he did, drinking the tart local wine in small gulps.

"Very unusual, I have never tasted anything like it."

"And you never will again."

"No—again is never like the first time." She suddenly was very much aware of his lips. They were so alive even when he was not eating or speaking. Neither too full nor too thin, they promised a feast for the senses. As if he could read her thoughts, he picked up her hand and kissed it. Her desire for his lips became even stronger. In vain, she tried to wash it away with the wine. She looked around. They had behaved as if they were quite alone. Indeed, all her colleagues had disappeared. Like locusts, they had come and gone leaving empty dishes and glasses behind.

"May I offer you a ride?"

Melissa was ready to accept anything he offered.

"Thank you. I guess we have to get back to the panel discussion. Are you on it?"

"No, are you?" They looked at each other knowing they would not go to the panel discussion. He led her to a battered red Porsche. When the engine hummed briefly and gave up, she wished that they could be stranded, but after toying with wires under the hood, he fixed it.

"They always give me cars that don't work," he growled as he maneuvered the narrow streets of the village, past the harbor and toward the coast. They both wore sunglasses. She could stare at him without being noticed. The three seductive lines at the corner of his mouth hinted at many secret encounters with women's lips. The hands that pressed gently against the wheel told his command of whatever he touched. Relaxed, he took each curve with care and ease. Comfortable with danger, he sometimes pushed forward playfully to take a hill with daring speed; at others he held back to lean into a curb or coast down to a steep gully. Then he would drive hard through a tunnel or straddle the edge of a dangerous abyss. The bucket seat kept her at a distance, but she yearned to reach over and caress his lips.

Impatiently he scanned the steep cliffs for access to the beach. At the mouth of a river, he followed a bumpy road down to a fine stretch of sand, protected by rocks on one side and palm trees on the other. From the trunk of the car he conjured up a bottle of wine and large colorful scarf. Where had the scarf come from, Melissa wondered. Did he keep it in the car for such occasions? Had another woman left it behind?

He spread the magenta-colored silk over a sheltered sand pit. The bright yellow and orange butterflies woven into the fabric scintillated in the sun as if they were alive. Close to them, the surf crashed against the rocks, and the foamy waves curled toward them into the sand. Pulling her close, he slowly unbuttoned her blouse and peeled her free of her slacks. In black bikini and bra she stretched out on the silky scarf soaking in the late afternoon sun. She was proud of her athletic, trim body and her small, girlish breasts. She was glad she had put on her luxury underwear. He said something in Spanish; she squinted at him against the glaring sun. For a long time he just stood there, staring at her. No man had ever looked at her like that. Self-consciously she closed her eyes.

When she opened them again to see what he was doing, he had disappeared. Why was he behaving so strangely? What did he intend to do? Suddenly her forty years turned back to fourteen. A Greek chorus of aunts and teachers and novelists were whispering unforgettable precautions: Never be alone with a stranger—never take your clothes off—never give in to lust—never trust a man—never travel alone in a foreign country—never go to the beach by yourself.

She pulled the scarf up around her hips and reached for her clothes. Then she saw him in the water. Like Poseidon he emerged from the ocean. His nutmeg-colored skin glistened, and tiny pearls of water dropped from his thighs. She had never seen such magnificent, frightening beauty. His torso was perfectly proportioned, his limbs exquisitely balanced, and then there was his cock. It stood out straight like a weapon, clearly aimed at her—she pulled back, disturbed, yet spellbound. "I've brought on this transformation. It is me he wants. I have that power over him," she thought. He knelt down beside her, again talking to himself in Spanish as his hands moved over her breasts and between her legs. There was a blessed silence as his lips began to travel from the tip of her toes upward inside her thighs.

"Come," she cried, "come to me now." But he took his time.

"First I enjoy you, then I enjoy myself." He offered her a gulp of wine. "The first time is very special. It is a coming together of strangers, we salute each other, recognize each other. Everything about you is new, your skin, your smell, your taste. Your voice too, the voice of passion. I have not heard it. Look at me, yes, go on. Talk to me, to my body, not to my brain."

Her eyes feasted on his muscular arms, the narrow hips, the strong hairy thighs. Her hands reached around his firmly rounded buttocks—as smooth and hairless as a baby's. But she could not express that sensation in words. She did not know his language, nor could she find her own. Against her pelvis pulsated his erection with a life of its own. She had always tried to ignore this most obtrusive male appendage. Now she ran her fingers over the throbbing vein; it felt so smooth and vulnerable that she wanted to draw it into her womb. Licking its silky tip, she tasted ocean and honey and man and life.

He gasped as if in pain. She could no longer control the rolling movements of her pelvis.

"I want you, I want you!" she cried out, giving herself totally to that new sensation of lust, of shameless greed for his beautiful body. He did not launch himself at her as she expected, but penetrated slowly, deliberately giving her time to feel him inside her. Then he was tossing her about like a raft on wild water. For a time she lost her own course. Happily she bounced along with him, but then she climbed on top to ride him, driving him close to delirium until she got her full measure of delight. Exhausted and content, she put her head on his chest, bathing her skin in the dew of their lovemaking, utterly relaxed and at peace. The sound of the ocean and from time to time his voice kept her entranced until she lost all consciousness in a mysterious, dream-filled sleep.

They missed the panel discussion and they missed their planes, but eventually they returned home to do everything that they were supposed to do. Claudio Torres de Valle won the Nobel Prize. Dr. Bingham duly gave her report of the conference and filed it away. Her life went on as usual, but at the most inappropriate times, in the middle of a committee meeting or a scientific presentation, that Spanish voice would ring in her ears, that nutmeg skin would glisten seductively before her eyes, and slowly her pelvis would begin to rock. She was riding the leopard.

Sabina's Scampi à la Leopard

The very essence of this culinary treat is that you don't cook it yourself and that you taste it far away from home. The circumstances are as important as the food and are thus beyond your control, no matter how well you plan ahead. Should you be lucky enough to succeed the first time, as I did, take my advice and do not try again.

I flew to Greece and found my way to the ancient harbor of Piraeus, which is an adventure if you are driving alone. When the ocean and boats came into view, I kept going higher along the edge of the cliff until I smelled the charcoal fires and saw the gigantic tentacles of octopus that hung from wooden trellises. I parked my car and strolled along the row of open-air tavernas until I found the one with the most spectacular view and the largest prawns roasting over the open fires. The tantalizing flavor of the broiled crustaceans already seduced my senses as I inhaled the smoke over a glass of ouzo.

I watched the young waiter as he pierced the plump morsels with a spit and held them over the glowing coals. The satisfaction on his face told me he knew why I had come from so far away. He put the scampi on my plate and smiled as if he had been waiting for me a long time. He watched me anxiously as I took the first bite. Our eyes met. Yes, it was perfect! His look trailed over my face toward my body, and I appraised his bronze chest and European shorts. He looked like Achilles, but he was no prince—just a fisherman. From inside the taverna came the sound of Greek music, not Zorba for the tourists but the sad wailing of Turkish melancholia that the Greeks play everywhere because life is so hard and what joy it offers comes now or never. Everything in Greece celebrates the past, nothing the future. I had been given the last gift of the god Neptune. I wouldn't be back—that would be greedy—but I would remember the taste forever.

If I had been wise, I would have left it at that. But of course I wasn't. Once I had tasted the food of the gods, I wanted more, an old story. I expected to find it on the menu of our hotel at the Gulf of Corinth. The waiter smiled indulgently, shaking his head; no, never, only at the harbor and even there their freshness wasn't guaranteed. They had to be eaten right after they were caught. Toward the end of our stay he confided that he knew the right place, but only for locals, not for tourists. He would take me himself because women did not go there alone. No, I couldn't bring the children; they wouldn't serve until ten in the evening. That's when I should meet him at the beach below the hotel.

By then I was so obsessed with the promise of scampi that no tourists had ever tasted, ones even better than those I had eaten before, that I deserted my two small children. I left them asleep in the hotel room and told nobody where I was going. The craving for scampi obliterated all other instincts as I crept out the door toward the abandoned stretch of sand where he was waiting.

Silently he walked in front of me. I had enough sense to stay behind, but not a soul could have heard me if I had cried for help. After about a mile, which seemed more like ten, we arrived at the dimly lit taverna. Everyone watched our entrance. I was the only woman among a motley assortment of Greeks who looked as if they had spent their lives on the water.

The prawns arrived—fifteen huge creatures in their shell, and indeed they tasted even better than the ones in Piraeus. He didn't eat but watched me solemnly.

"Very good," I said.

He nodded. His English was rudimentary. What did he expect of me? His handsome face was closed. Suddenly I felt like an American. I thought of my children alone in the room. What if they woke and couldn't find me? I thought of his wife, the old cook who wasn't all that old, but who worked twelve hours in the hotel kitchen and then some

74

more at home, a shack in our courtyard where her children sometimes played with mine.

I couldn't finish the prawns. All I wanted was to go back to the hotel. He seemed disappointed but ate what I had left on my plate while I talked nonstop about my wonderful husband who would pick us up the next day and about my children who might wonder where I was. He understood and called for the bill. Naïvely, I had surmised that we would eat for free among his friends. But they treated him like a tourist. I offered to pay. He tossed his head back—an indignant Greek denial. I thanked him profusely—too profusely? What did he expect in return?

We walked back the same way we had come, but this time I hurried ahead, consumed with anxiety about the children. He trailed further and further behind. The distance between us became as great as that between our countries.

The children had not even changed their positions. I breathed a deep sigh of relief. From my window I noticed the light shining from the open doorway of the shack in the courtyard. The old cook was sitting on the step waiting for her husband to come home.

Queen of the Road

fat: in good shape; hauling a big load
—*CBer's Atlas and Dictionary* (1976)

Five more chocolates . . . then it would be time to go. Ava reached furtively to the back of her desk drawer and found a chocolate almondette, her favorite. She held it in her hand a moment to warm it, then quietly removed the cellophane wrapper and placed the candy on her tongue, letting it linger there as long as possible. Ava was not the sort to bite and gobble a chocolate or to eat more than one at a time. Pleasures, like chocolates, were not to be rushed, but parceled out carefully, one by one, so that a constant stream of taste would last forever.

Ava glanced out of her narrow office window. Far below, on the freeway snaking out from the city, she could see the cars already strung together like beads on a necklace. She could hardly wait to be among them. Rush hour was her favorite time, and Ava savored her commute as secretly as she savored her forbidden chocolates.

Ever since Ava had bought the car of her dreams soon after her promotion, her life had changed dramatically. She suddenly felt part of the "Pepsi generation"—alive and sparkling just like everyone on television. In an instant the purchase of a Honda did everything that a lifetime of unsuccessful dieting had not. Once inside the car she was as small and agile as everyone else. With no effort on her part she could move with spring and zest, bounding like a jackrabbit with just the slightest touch of the accelerator. She loved cutting through heavy traffic, squeezing in and out of the smallest parking places, and soaring the skyways like a weightless cosmonaut. How coordinated and light she had become! The Honda made her feel like a ballerina pirouetting in a size three tutu.

In addition to her new sense of mobility, Ava experienced an anonymity that her large size had always deprived her of. Unseen in the snug driver's seat, she was no longer the object of other people's stares, and for the first time felt free to gaze at them instead. To her amazement she saw an array of unselfconscious behavior far more revealing than anything she could watch on television or read about in magazines. Drivers seemed to think they were invisible, and Ava delighted in observing them.

Sometimes she would spot an appealing man traveling alone and would follow his car for miles, creating his life story and imagining a passionate meeting between them. More frequently, though, Ava searched for lovers, seeking some clue about what she was missing, hoping to find the kind of affectionate rapport she yearned for.

Sadly, the couples she found did not often answer her need. The well-dressed pairs in BMWs talked enough but usually sat too far apart. The wholesome ones in Volvos that sported "No Nuke" bumper stickers chatted with the most animation, but Ava guessed that their talk was too issue-oriented for romance. The entwined lovers in low-riders didn't count because they were too young and vigorous and totally beyond her ilk. The same was true for couples huddled together on motorcycles. RV drivers were another category she excluded: the pairs in front always sat apart, pale and silent, exhausted from the effort of dragging family and paraphernalia to and from crowded campsites. If there ever was any visible interaction, it was usually one of the parents swatting a crying child.

Occasionally, though, Ava would find what she was looking for: a couple about her own age sitting close and radiating an affection that filled her with longing. Just that morning on her way to work Ava had seen such a pair ahead of her in line at the toll booth. The woman drove dreamily with her male companion sitting close. She wore only a sleeveless jersey despite the cold fog, but Ava imagined that their bed warmth still encased her. A huge barrette held her torrent of hair, and the man's left hand played with those loose curls on her neck. Ava's own hairs had stood up, aroused. Did the woman wear perfume? Underwear? The man moved closer and kissed her ear, and Ava felt a blush upon her own cheek as a shiver streaked across her shoulders.

This evening before leaving work Ava spent more time than usual in the women's room. She always groomed herself meticulously before the long ride home, but tonight she experimented with a new upswept hairdo, something like the one the woman had been wearing that morning. During lunch, she had purchased two bright plastic combs, which held her hair in soft waves away from her face. The new hairdo revealed her dangling earrings and accentuated the fleshy curve of her neck. Ava smiled and hurried for the elevator with her car keys already in hand.

In her Honda and on her way at last, Ava hoped for a traffic jam, but the cars on the freeway approach were moving normally. Suddenly a truck without its trailer cut close in front. Sparks flew from a chain that dragged from its connecting cable, and black smoke belched from its smokestack. Ava braked and honked angrily. The driver's beefy elbow hung out the window. Then his muscular arm straightened and, reaching out, motioned her to pass.

Ava gunned her engine and tore past the nuisance, cutting in this time on him. Just as she was claiming a moral victory, the cab swung out and pulled up parallel. The roar of its engine was deafening, so Ava dropped back. With a fresh toot the cab again cut in front. The big arm reached out the window and adjusted the side mirror. As it moved, she thought she saw the driver's flashing smile. Then he raised his hand and waved to her.

The traffic in the left lane was moving faster now, so Ava took advantage of the opportunity to get a better glimpse. As she came alongside the cab, she could see only the top of its huge wheels from her little Honda. She decided to cut in front and watch the trucker in her rearview mirror. By the time she had him in focus, his head was thrown back in laughter. In a moment he was switching lanes and was overtaking her. He honked three times as he thundered past. Not to be outdone, Ava immediately accelerated, this time passing him on the right.

Their game of leapfrog continued for several miles. She was unaware of the flush on her cheek and the smile on her lips, oblivious even to the fact that she had overshot her exit. She focused only on out-maneuvering the jaunty cab, which was amazingly agile without its load. They roared neck and neck down the two center lanes, each daring the other to pull back first. Suddenly the Honda jerked and ground sharply to the right. With all her strength and skill Ava brought her swerving car to a safe stop on the shoulder of the freeway.

Ava climbed out, rather shaken, and walked to the right side of the car. The front wheel was completely flat.

"Oh damn," she muttered. She had never changed a tire.

As she gazed at the shimmering freeway wondering what to do, she saw the cab pull off about a half-mile beyond. The trucker in his white T-shirt and jeans was running back to her. Ava beamed with relief.

"You okay?" he called.

"Yes. I just have a flat tire."

He was beside her now, panting a bit, and quite burly and tan.

"I didn't push you off the road now, did I?" he asked with a wink.

"Oh, you wouldn't do a thing like that!" she played along.

"Here, I'll change it for you, little lady."

Ava almost laughed aloud. Little lady! She opened the trunk to get the spare.

"Look! It's flat, too," the trucker said cheerfully. "We'll get it filled. Grab your purse and come with me."

"Hey, thanks," cried Ava, genuinely grateful.

"You deserve some kind of break. My God, I've never seen anyone drive like you. Now be careful in those little shoes along the side here. It's full of broken glass."

He guided her by the elbow along the garbage-strewn rubble. Ava felt like a dainty geisha hobbling beside him. He walked with long strides. Ava like that, even though it was an effort to keep up. The tire in his outer hand looked as small and light as a frisbee. When they reached the cab, he swung the door open for her. Ava hesitated at the insurmountable step. She would have to lift her skirt to her waist and find handholds to even attempt it. She felt panicky.

Suddenly the trucker's hands were upon her waist, and before she could scream, "Stop! You can't!" he had hoisted her to the seat. Her heart pounded. She had never been picked up like that before. She sat like a startled canary just captured and plopped in a cage. While she tottered breathlessly on her new perch straightening her feathers and trying to find her voice again, her bold handler mounted the driver's seat. She peered cautiously at him to see if he was unhurt after lifting her so rashly. He was only of average height and stocky build, definitely not a weight-lifter. He smiled back at her.

"Well, how d'ya like it?"

"I'm just amazed!" exclaimed Ava. Then, turning her wonder from trucker to cab, her eyes grew wide as she took in the confusion of knobs, switches, and buttons. "I've never seen anything like this!"

The cab was immaculate and spacious. It smelled faintly of vinyl and sun lotion. The bench seat was firm and smooth. It did not hug her like the bucket seat in the Honda. The freedom to move about made Ava a little giddy.

The trucker relished her interest.

"Just watch," he laughed and flicked on the ignition. The dashboard lit up blue. "By the way, I'm Louie."

"Hi, I'm Ava."

"Now, Ava," he spoke her name as though he'd been using it all along, "when that light goes off, you rev 'er up . . . like this." He turned the key another notch, and the deep-throated diesel began to cough and rattle. Louie gunned the motor a couple of times and shifted into low gear. The brakes released with a hiss, and the cab quivered as he waited for an opening in the traffic. Ava's enameled nails dug into her purse. With a lurch the cab accelerated. She leaned forward and watched the pavement zipping by directly below. Strangely, the absence of a hood did not make her feel unprotected; nothing could harm her in this high seat. As Louie careened into the faster lanes, Ava looked down into the laps of other drivers.

"You only get to see the knees from up here," she declared.

"You bet, and a lot of thigh! Just look at those seat covers over there!" crowed Louie. He pointed to a trim pair of cutoffs to Ava's right.

"To tell the truth," he continued, "I prefer yours. I like a curvaceous thigh."

"Why, you lousy rubbernecker! Just what I'd expect from a trucker!" she laughed.

"Oh, I'm a connoisseur of fine thighs, and I like a lady who keeps herself up the way you do."

A loud garbled voice broke in. Louie picked a mike from the dashboard.

"Howzit?"

"Hit me one time."

"Make your mark."

"How copy."

"Bodacious, Red Rascal. You're meltin' the voice coil."

"10-45."

"Negatory. 10-6."

"Rodger-dodger!"

"Ten out."

Louie hung up.

"That tearjerker's been scannin' the Band all day." He glanced at Ava. "CB talk," he explained.

"I didn't get a word."

"It's a cinch once you get the hang of it."

"At least you know you're not out here alone."

"For sure, but this ain't the time to chew the fat. I don't catch foxes in distress every day." Louie winked at her, but Ava was examining the panel.

"You like my goodies? Here, try these." Louie handed her a pair of headphones and pointed to his tape deck.

Ava laughed. "All the comforts of home!"

"Just look behind you."

Ava turned around and lifted up a curtain.

"My goodness! A bed! But where's the rest of your truck?"

"You mean that ain't enough? You want a bathroom and a TV room and a kitchen?"

Ava shrieked with laughter. "No, you know, that other part."

"My rig. She's loadin' up in Vacaville."

She? wondered Ava.

"How big is *she*?"

"Oh, about twenty tons and all of it cherries!" Louie exploded with mirth.

"Is it hard to move that much?"

"Naw, it's not so much the weight but the distribution. You gotta pack it right."

How true, thought Ava, and she smoothed her skirt over her generous thighs.

"Here we are," announced Louie. "I'll duck out and fill your spare."

He leaped out and was at the air hose in what looked like one simple movement. Though not a large man, Louie was compact and well proportioned. Ava admired the firm curve of his back as he leaned over the pump. In the dim twilight his T-shirt looked even whiter than before, as though it would glow in the dark. She thought everything about him gleamed with vitality, and she wondered why someone so agile would want to drive a truck.

As if to answer her own question, Ava sidled over to his seat. She took the big, flat steering wheel in her hands and placed her feet on the pedals. A sudden sense of power impelled her to blow the horn.

Louie came running back and jumped in the passenger's side.

"Okay, Ava babe, take 'er away."

Ava broke into gales of laughter.

"C'mon, I'll show you. Here, start 'er like I showed you."

"But the gears . . ."

"Why, hon, there's only thirteen forward ones," teased Louie. "You're in neutral, so start . . . that's right. Now release the brake and drop 'er into low . . . there . . . that one . . . no, down more." Louie placed his hand over hers on the gearshift and guided it to the right notch. The cab groaned and jerked.

"Don't tense. When I say '*now*,' do the clutch just like you're used to and I'll help you with the stick. *Now!*"

Ave shifted into the next gear, and they crawled forward.

"*Now!*" Again they shifted.

"*Now!* Good! I knew you'd catch on fast. *Now!* Hang a left at the corner, and you'll be on the overpass back to the freeway."

Once Ava reached a cruising speed she began to relax. She smiled at Louie, who watched her proudly. From time to time he patted her hand.

"You look awful good . . . just like you belong," he purred in a low voice.

Ava grew aware of her breasts. Either the vibration of the road or Louie's gaze upon them made them perk up. The hard ride caused them to jiggle.

"You sure do get the feel of the road in these seats!" said Ava, trying to distance herself.

"Oh, yeah. You get a good ride," agreed Louie.

And then in her nervousness Ava accidentally ran the left tires along the lane divider buttons, causing her heart as well as her breasts to palpitate.

"Whoa!" she cried. "This is better than a Jacuzzi!"

Louie laughed.

"You ought to drive the whole rig. She's a real hummer! Want to come with me?"

Ava looked at him and said in a teasing voice, "Can't you see I'm busy driving? I don't need a man."

"Look, honey, you drive long enough and you'll *want* a man. I can do more for you than any eighteen-wheeler."

"Like what?"

"Oh, give you a good time. I mean it. Anytime you want to run a rig with me, just holler."

Louie took his hand off hers and reached deep into a pocket. He brought out his card and slipped it into her hand. Ava glanced at it and smiled at him. The laugh lines around his lips were deeply etched, rugged and kind. She liked his expressive, smiling eyes. He was active and virile, the type of man that Ava often admired from afar.

Louie draped his arm over the back of her seat and gently touched the nape of her neck. Ava's customary impulse to deflect him with a joke suddenly left her. His touch was gentle, tender, much more refined, in fact, than his talk. They rode along in comfortable silence. A road sign warned "Soft Shoulder" just as Louie fondled hers. Ava smiled to herself, remembering other cautions of the road: "Right of Way," "Yield," "Slippery When Wet."

Louie squeezed her shoulder and sighed reluctantly.

"We have to head for the next exit if you want to get back to your car. I'll help you downshift." He put his hand over hers again.

Ava smiled at him and pressed the clutch. Louie guided her hand on the stick shift. With each change of gear the cab bucked and groaned in an ever-deepening protest that matched her own. Ava felt like a helpless child again, hating the magical merry-go-round ride to end.

"Easy, easy," soothed Louie.

"I wish I could drive a rig," Ava sighed.

"Well, why don't you? It's a great living—always moving and changing. I could give you some lessons when I finish my run."

"You mean it?"

"Sure I do. But first you'll have to get a permit." While he told her how to do this, he motioned her to steer toward an overpass that returned them to the other side of the freeway. When Ava's crippled Honda came into view on the shoulder ahead, Louie helped her ease the cab off the road. It began to buck and lurch.

"Hit the clutch!" he cried, too late. The cab had already stalled with a final snort. Louie threw on the hand brake and the emergency lights and opened the door. "Good enough," he said as he jumped out and turned with outstretched arms for her.

Ava slid across the seat and allowed him to help her to the ground. This time he held her close and lowered her so slowly that she could feel her skirt riding up as it passed over his body—first rippling across the muscled bulges beneath his T-shirt, then catching on his warm metal belt buckle, before coming to rest in a rumpled heap against his rock-hard quadriceps. She thought her knees would buckle from desire and was glad that he held her a moment longer.

"Atta way," he murmured when he was sure she had found her footing. Then he took her hand in one of his, grabbed the tire in the other, and walked her back to her car. He changed the flat in no time, giving her pointers every step of the way so that she wouldn't be help-less if it happened again. He held the car door open for her as she got in. Cars flashed by behind him, so near that Ava could feel the hot blasts of air in their wake.

"Be careful," she cried.

"Don't worry," he shrugged, but he closed the door and sidled closer, hovering over the open window. "Don't you forget to get a per-mit," he added.

Ava laughed. She hardly needed a reminder. She squeezed the steering wheel with a surge of pleasure. Her hand still clutched Louie's card. The dampness of her palm had molded it into a tight curl.

"Wait a minute!" he continued suddenly. "How am I ever going to find you?"

The alarm in his voice touched her, and she answered, "Look under Swanson—in the Oakland phone book."

"Okay now, you be good. No more drag racing 'til I get back, hear?"

"Well, you better hurry!"

"Give me three weeks—just three weeks," he begged. Then he smiled seductively and stroked her cheek with the back of his hand before locking her door protectively and stepping out of the way. In a daze Ava took off with tires screeching. She glanced in the rearview mirror and saw Louie waving her on. She swelled with excitement to think of taking him on in an eighteen-wheeler.

Class of '83

At the Royal Surf everything was true travel-poster Polynesian. The Pacific crashed dramatically against the black rocks. Torches illuminated the winding paths bordered by ferns and banana trees to guide happy couples from the Tonga Bar to the pool or to their authentically thatched bungalows. The Tonga Bar, like the Coral Reef restaurant and the lobby, opened on one side toward the ocean, on the other toward the tropical gardens.

The band was playing "Red Roses for a Blue Lady." Sheila remembered that tonight was "Fifties Night" and wished that Tom were with her so they could boogie. The dance floor was full. It took her a while to realize that all the couples belonged to her parents' generation. The ladies in blue-gray curls or platinum wigs had donned flowered muumuus, and the gentlemen matched them with Hawaiian shirts. Their identical leis gave them away as a group. At the Royal Surf one walked, dined, and danced in pairs, unless one belonged to a particular constellation known as a "party." At the registration desk, single travelers were funneled into organized fun by travel agents and recreation managers to maximize the efficient distribution of money and pleasure.

The bell captain spotted Sheila as a single guest occupying an ocean-front room with a king-size bed, and right away the Royal Surf hostess had pressed a free drink into her hand and directed her to the Aloha cocktail party where other singles were already waiting for a match.

"I am expecting my husband," Sheila had protested. Every day she fought for isolation as assorted fellow singles tried to invade her private space at the table or poolside. She soon became known as the "lady who's waiting for her husband."

Tonight, she had hoped to sit quietly in the back of the bar sipping her daiquiri, but a Hawaiian shirt was already advancing toward her. Sheila braced herself. She found it so difficult to be rude. How could she refuse an old man? Of course she agreed to dance with him. He reminded her of her father. Not only was he her father's exact age, as it turned out, but also a retired colonel. He used the same language with the same authority and moved with that familiar mixture of dash and dignity. A skillful dancer and proud of it, he pressed her close without missing a beat.

"My children have given me this trip for my seventieth birthday," he confessed, "and I'm having a splendid time. I should have done this years ago when my wife was alive, but she didn't like to travel. She'd had enough of it in the army."

Sheila told him that her children had also presented her with this trip to Hawaii, all paid for from their summer jobs and savings.

"You're just a kid yourself—class of '83?" he boldly tapped the inscription on her U.C. T-shirt.

Sheila blushed. "It's sort of a joke. My boys and I all go to college now. I never finished school." She started to tell him about Peter and Chris at college, and about Kate and Kevin, the twins still living at home, when he interrupted her, nodding discreetly toward a woman who tried her best to resemble Carol Channing.

"My sweetheart," he said. "Isn't she something? She's only fifty-five and as strong as a horse. We do all the Air Force exercises together. We'll get married as soon as we get back to Long Beach. Heck, I thought my life was over, but look at me now!" His hand moved down Sheila's spine.

"Isn't your fiancée waiting for you?" Sheila asked, eager to be rid of him.

"She's mad as hell at me. You see, I make her jealous from time to time; it does wonders for her in bed." Like Sheila's father the colonel enjoyed talking, and, again like her father, his conversation always drifted in one direction like river water.

Sheila finally made her escape into the darkness of the deserted beach. She could still hear the band playing "Love Me Tender." Would she and Tom be dancing together at seventy? "I'll join you as soon as I can get away," he had promised when she left. He liked to give the impression that the business was on the point of collapse, that he was holding up the crumbling roof with one hand while keeping the wolf away from the door with the other. Occasionally he would announce his intention of starting a new life. It always sounded like a threat, as if a "new life" meant something terrible. "Let's just go away for a few days," she would suggest.

"Sure," he would say, "but not now."

She never made a scene. For Sheila, scenes were bad habits, like chewing with one's mouth open. If only she could reach out to him, but she feared that even the slightest move might cause a break. The children knew it. Romance would bring them back together, she hoped.

When she was honest with herself, she wished Tom would not come at all. What if they were to spend every night staring at their fragile marriage suspended between them—two mummies on top of a king-size bed, entombed inside their ocean-front room? Strangely she no longer felt alarmed about Tom. Perhaps it was the air. The intoxicating perfume of the plumeria and the sound of the ocean soothed her anxiety. The warm, slightly damp atmosphere made her feel protected like a hothouse plant. Stretching out in the beach chair, she gazed into the moonlit water. Something moved in the surf. It was huge. She sat up trying to make out what it was—a fish? No, two fish, two huge creatures splashing around in the silvery crest.

"They come every night," said a voice behind her. "You can see better from over there." The boy beckoned her to follow him. Now she recognized his face. She had noticed him at dinner where he also ate alone. His white cutoffs stood out against his deeply tanned legs. His very blond hair contrasted with the tone of his skin. He could be one of the teenage crowd that spilled in and out of Sheila's house every day. He was carrying a bucket.

"Come and watch." He motioned her again toward a rocky, narrow ridge which extended like a natural pier into the ocean. Curious, she scrambled after him.

"Want one?" He offered her a piece of fish from his bucket. "Manta rays. I feed them every night. We keep it a secret, or the tourists would chase them away."

"You live here then? I thought you were a guest at the Surf."

"Well, I guess I am. I come here on holidays with my father. He has a suite. His firm built the Surf." He grinned. "I've seen you too. I like your shirt. I'm supposed to go to Cal in the fall."

"We may run into each other then."

"The truth is, I don't want to go. I don't like school. How about you? I guess nobody's making you go."

"You're right. It's something I've been wanting to do for many years."

"Why?" He seemed perplexed.

"Well, I get time to think. I get to read a lot of books that I have always wanted to read. And I meet new people who are interested in ideas, *my* ideas. I even get a chance to write them down."

He looked at her as if she was speaking a foreign language. Sheila was surprised to hear herself talk this way to a boy. It was the first time that she had come up with a clear statement of why she had wanted to go back to school. Maybe it was the strangeness of the situation, the balmy night, the remoteness. Maybe it was the boy's way of looking at her so directly. He tossed another fish into the water. Then she took over. By the time they had emptied the bucket, there were at least five mantas in the sea.

"Watch!" He suddenly stepped toward the edge of the rock. She gasped as he dived into the whirl of moving fins.

"The sharks," she shouted after him, but of course he could not hear her through the surf. His white shorts bobbed up and down in the dark water as he tried to take hold of a flopping saucer shape. After a good deal of splashing, he reappeared on the rock.

"There's one that lets me ride him, but I couldn't find him," he explained offhandedly.

"Isn't that terribly dangerous?" she asked.

"I've been in that water since I was four, and I'm still here, right? Sharks don't come to this cove. I don't know why, but they don't; they go over there to the harbor. Sharks hang out in the same area most of the time—mantas are like dolphins, they like to play." He obviously was showing off. Sheila was glad that he was not hers, that she had no obligation to correct him, and that she need not worry about him. She could simply watch him like another creature of the island. When he invited her to go sailing the next morning, she agreed easily.

Half expecting him not to be there, she arrived late at the marina. But he had readied the catamaran and was chatting with a group of teenagers. Casually he waved her on board as if they had done this many times before. Then it occurred to Sheila that the boy was only doing his job. She wondered how much he would charge, but couldn't bring herself to ask. Matt didn't look like the usual tourist pleaser; perhaps he would be offended. Sheila longed to be out there in the blue haze, whatever the cost.

To his surprise, she was a pretty good sailor. They took turns at the rudder until they reached the lagoon. Since she had never snorkled before, Matt showed her how to breathe through the tube and how to kick with her flippers. Then, without further ceremony, he pushed her off the side. If she was scared, she didn't show it, no silly giggles or affected screams. But when he joined her in the water, she stayed close behind him, trusting him to be her guide.

For Sheila, the world below the choppy blue surface surpassed all expectations. Whatever she had anticipated, she did not imagine this underwater garden of black and white coral and pink and green seaweed surrounded by blue parrot fish and hundreds of small yellow butterfly fish. When Matt crumbled a piece of bread into the water, they all came toward him like pigeons in the park. The dark crags of reef scared her, especially when his finger pointed to the fierce-looking face of a moray eel, but somehow she felt accepted by nature. They were two human shapes in the seascape floating among many other shapes, curious about each other, but not threatening.

From time to time Sheila's body brushed against Matt's. It was a comforting, friendly sensation; at the same time she was aware of his maleness, his long, muscular thighs, his narrow hips. She caught herself staring at him from behind her mask as she would never have dared on shore.

Back on board she felt suddenly embarrassed as if she had seen him naked, which in a sense was true. His bathing trunks did not conceal very much. She wondered if he would try to kiss her and if she would let him. But he busied himself with a picnic basket from which he produced two beautifully wrapped gourmet sandwiches and a bottle of wine. Sheila was touched by his thoughtfulness. When had anyone made a sandwich for her? Come to think of it, when had anyone arranged a whole day for her pleasure? That was her role at home: packing picnics, arranging outings, and making everybody happy.

They grinned a little sheepishly at each other while they ate. Sex was there, she knew it and guessed that he knew it, but neither one was ready to handle that possibility. Matt pointed toward a palm-lined lagoon. "My father is trying to buy that piece of beach over there, not for himself, mind you, for his company. It has the best stretch of sand on this side of the island. It belongs to an old Hawaiian guy—to his family actually—but he lives there alone, plants taro and goes fishing. Anybody he likes can use the fish for free. He gives you fish and fruit, everything. They've offered him a million dollars, but he says he doesn't need it."

"Most people never know what they need," she replied.

"Do you?" His question surprised her. Unlike her own sons and his teenage friends he seemed to be seriously interested in her opinions. Sheila felt comfortable enough to answer him honestly.

"I thought so once. Now I'm no longer so sure. Perhaps I'm like that Hawaiian guy. I wouldn't have exchanged my house for anything in the world when the kids were younger, when I was taking care of them. Now I wish I could take care of myself. Even here, I keep looking for things to do with my husband—I mean after he gets here, things that he would enjoy."

"Like snorkeling?" Sheila could see that Matt was offended.

"What about your mother?" Sheila asked cautiously.

"She's just like my father. I don't know why they didn't stay together; they both talk money. She runs a couple of sports shops in Tahoe. She never leaves, winter or summer. Her lawyer is always after my father's lawyer; they never stop."

When they returned to shore in the evening, they knew a lot about each other. For one, he was waiting for his father, and she was waiting for her husband. Sheila could not forget what he had said about his father. It reminded her disturbingly of Tom: "My father likes the *idea* of me. He always tells me what we are going to do together, but he never does it. He always has some important deal coming up. If I didn't show, he would be upset of course." Sheila looked forward to continuing the conversation at dinner. She dressed carefully, anticipating sharing the evening with a companion.

But Matt did not show up at the restaurant. The mahimahi tasted bland. The wine was too sweet. The sun-blistered faces annoyed her. What did she have in common with them? And what did Matt have in common with them? From his point of view, she was probably just another member of the adult world that had let him down. He had told her proudly that he had plenty of friends, both haole and Hawaiian. Perhaps momentarily he had been drawn toward the mirage of a mother-friend, but his interests must lie elsewhere. She supposed he was avoiding her because he was embarrassed about the afternoon. Sheila tried to laugh at herself, but, like a slight yet persistent headache, her disappointment intruded and clouded her usual evening stroll. She ended up at the shopping mall trying on bathing suits designed for Bo Derek.

Matt saw Sheila leave the restaurant. She looked like a girl with her white slacks and dark glasses, her shoulder-length brown hair tied back with a scarf. He cursed himself for having wasted so much time shaving and picking his clothes, especially since he had opted for a pair of faded jeans and his favorite old tennis shirt. His plan had been to casually join her at the table and then, just as casually, to take her to a movie. Too late. For awhile he followed her around, hoping that she would run into him, but he knew that he no longer had the courage to ask her out. She probably took him for a beach bum or worse.

Suddenly he thought of a new tactic. As soon as she disappeared into the Beachcomber Boutique, he headed for her room. It was easy to get a master key. He knew the hotel inside and out and often pitched in for the bellboy. Once she found him in her room, she would get mad and throw him out, or...! In his fantasy he was James Bond. He'd search her room. He'd know all about her before he made his move.

Everything in her room was disappointingly neat and tidy. Sheila was not the kind of person to toss her shoes on the floor or leave her clothes carelessly strewn about. Only a white nightgown laid out on the bed gave her presence away. Matt picked it up and inhaled her perfume. A look behind the sliding mirror of the closet revealed an array of dresses. Orange and yellow seemed to be her favorite colors, but he had never seen her wear any of these elegant numbers. For a moment he saw her on his arm in a canary chiffon gown as they entered the exclusive King Kamehameha Club. The maître d' showed them to their table, the headwaiter stooped over Matt's shoulder with the wine list, and he ordered French champagne. Then he reminded himself that her dresses were obviously waiting for the son-of-a-bitch husband. Still he continued his investigation, opening every drawer and examining its contents: beach paraphernalia, cosmetics, some college textbooks and a lot of paperbacks by authors he had never heard of, and—of course—her underwear. He could not resist going back to that particular drawer. Running his fingers over the sheer lace, the smooth satin, he imagined his hands inside her panties.

Suddenly he heard the key in the door. Panic. He forgot all about his plan. Quickly he flicked on the television and huddled himself in the armchair pretending to watch.

"What are you doing here?" Sheila asked in surprise and a bit sternly. She turned off the set. Guiltily, Matt scrambled to his feet. "I only wanted to say good night."

"Good night." He didn't budge. She said it again, more kindly. She realized his panic at having been caught. To help him, now that she had recovered, she kissed him lightly—maternally she thought—on the cheek. But her heart stopped, then pounded fiercely. In his hand he was clutching her panties. To her consternation, she found that sight very exciting. His hunger for her was so obvious and yet so innocent. It made him irresistible. She put down her parcels and purse and unbuttoned her blouse. Then everything happened with lightning speed. Within seconds they were out of their clothes and in bed together, and it was over just as quickly.

"My," she said, "do you always gobble everything up so fast?"

"I was afraid you'd change your mind."

"Tell you what, let me get some sleep and tomorrow we'll try again—my way, okay?"

"Can't I stay?"

Before she could answer, the telephone rang. Hastily, she pulled on her bathrobe, suddenly self-conscious of her nakedness. Matt could tell that it was her husband at the other end of the line. Still cursing himself for his clumsiness, he decided that things couldn't get any worse, so he stayed in the room. The conversation was brief and one-sided.

"That's fine. Yes, I'll see you then," was all she said.

"Bad news?" Matt asked, reading her face.

"No, that was my husband. He says he'll be here tomorrow night." She seemed lost in thought. Matt went over to her and brushed her hair off her face, ready to say good-bye. She pulled his head down and kissed him. He kissed her breasts, and he buried his head in her lap. She let him stay there. After a while he asked if he could look at her. Her knees opened, parting the folds of her silk robe. He could see her pubic hair between her slender thighs and touched her soft petals, gently prying her apart like a rose.

"I like that," she whispered, "kiss me there."

He felt the moist folds, the different textures of flesh and skin and hair. She shivered and moaned, telling him when to stop and when to begin again. Finally, she whispered, "You see, I am learning too. Nobody has ever done this to me before."

Sheila wondered why it was so easy to tell Matt what she wanted. In all their years together, she had never managed to tell Tom. Guiding Matt's fingers, she made him listen to her breath, to every clue in giving her pleasure. She was his teacher, but she was also a student. There was so much she did not know about herself.

"Do you like this?" Matt asked again and again. His curiosity about her body never seemed satisfied. Tracing her hips and buttocks, he marveled at her curves, her finely chiseled bones, her tender skin. "Look at your nails," he exclaimed, "they are perfect, the shape, the nail polish, everything just right." And she rewarded him with a massage, proving what her fingers could do.

At some point when he was barely awake, Matt heard Shiela's voice speaking into the telephone, calmly informing her husband that it would be better if he did not come, that she needed more time for herself.

"I will be back next week," she said matter-of-factly. She hung up the phone pensively. Matt turned toward her and said, "I want to make it so good for you that you won't go."

From then on, they were inseparable. "How sweet," smiled the hotel guests, "such a nice mother and son. They do everything together."

When his friends had teased him about his affair with an "old lady," he had gotten into a fist fight. How could he explain to them what it meant to have someone who accepted him for what he was, who never put him down? Sheila had not even laughed at his art. When she had asked him why he drew only airplanes, she had sounded really interested, not critical. When they made love, she never held anything back from him. She was like no other girl he had ever known. She let him look at her as long as he liked until he knew every part of her. On their last night he wanted to kiss all of her good-bye. Sheila felt his tears on her shoulder. He told her that he loved her, that he couldn't bear to see her leave. Exhausted, she did not turn around. The next morning he was gone.

As the plane lifted off the ground, her spirits soared high. "I made love, I really made love," she proclaimed to herself. The cabin was packed with returning tourists. Across the aisle sat the colonel and his bride. Hungrily they tore into a bag of potato chips. They held hands. Each wore several leis. Sheila's lei came from a meadow near the lagoon where the old Hawaiian lived. Orchids grew wild there. Matt had gathered the blossoms and strung them for her.

The whole family met her at the airport. They couldn't see Sheila right away because she followed behind the happy couple. But then Kevin ran up to her. "Hi, Mom, did you have a good time? Did you bring me a piece of coral?" Tom stood back, apart from the others as if he expected to be brushed aside. She walked over to him and put the lei around her husband's neck.

Second Opinion

Ellen Rossiter was Harvey Rostow's final office patient late on a Friday evening. He had scheduled her at the last minute because her referring doctor was a good friend. Forewarned that she was blind, he went to the waiting room himself to get her and show her to his office. This simple act of courtesy impressed Ellen and put her at ease.

"Tell me," Dr. Rostow began as he guided her down the hall, "is it worse, do you think, to be blind from birth?"

"No, I don't," Ellen answered, surprised that this should be his first question. Most doctors seemed bound by their role to appear omniscient, to conceal their curiosity. "My friends who were once sighted have to learn what I know instinctively," she explained. "They translate everything from their lost sense."

"I can't imagine functioning without my sight," he confessed.

"You'd probably fare better than some, being a cardiologist. Your hearing must be well developed."

"Yes, with a stethoscope, but I'm not sure how much that would help get me around my kitchen or across a street," he laughed.

In his office now, seated on their respective sides of a massive desk, he continued in a more doctorly tone.

"Ms. Rossiter, or Ellen—which should I call you?"

"Ellen is fine."

"I understand from Dr. Lewis that you have been experiencing arrhythmias. Would you describe them, please?"

As she did, Ellen could hear his ballpoint pen making rapid notes. He enjoyed taking a history from such a bright, articulate patient. He watched her sitting across from him, calm and willowy in a soft knit dress that echoed the gray-blue of her eyes. Her hands lay quietly folded in her lap, and she looked at him with a steady, open gaze that radiated harmony and composure, a serenity that hours of primping before lighted mirrors would have destroyed, he was certain. Her finely tuned attention was so disturbing that he had to turn back to her record.

"I see that it's been almost a year since you were last examined, so I'd like to check you and then we'll talk. Let me show you to the examining room."

He stood beside her as she rose from her chair and took her by the hand to a small room farther down the hall. Ellen could tell from walking hand in hand beside him that he was quite tall and thin. Her hands wanted to move across his face and hair with the quivering energy of butterfly wings to seek more information, a frequent impulse that she had grown used to stifling.

The examining room smelled of the typical hospital blend: formica, linoleum, alcohol, and iodine. Dr. Rostow cupped her hand over a metal hook on the back of the door to show her where to hang her clothes, then pressed a disposable paper smock into her other hand before leaving.

Ellen undressed nervously, knowing that it was not dread of the impending examination that undid her. Here, unexpectedly, was a man who was compassionate, kind, and self-revealing. The combination of so many rare qualities in a *man* made Ellen wish to know him. She unfolded the stiff paper gown with difficulty. It stuck together, making it almost impossible to find the armholes, and when she finally got it on and hoisted herself up on the table, she worried that the smock was on upside down.

Dr. Rostow returned with an office nurse.

"Stay sitting up," he said. "We'll take your blood pressure and then examine your head and chest."

Ellen heard him go to a small sink in the corner of the room and start to wash his hands. The nurse slapped a blood pressure band on her upper arm, vigorously pumped as tight as it would go, and waited. With a sigh, the pressure eased, and Ellen could feel her circulation return.

"120 over 80," announced the nurse, tearing off the Velcro band with a loud rip. Ellen touched her upper arm to see if it was still intact.

Dr. Rostow came and stood before her. He took her hands in both of his and held them briefly, looking at the palms and nails. Ellen found it a most reassuring gesture regardless of its medical import. Then he held her face between his hands for a moment, and when he removed them, she felt the warmth still cupping her chin like two indelible handprints. Next the warm beam of the otoscope traveled deep inside her ears, then her nose, mouth, and eyes. Afterward, Ellen heard him dismantle the otoscope and put it away in a leather case that snapped shut. There was a pause, and then Dr. Rostow's smooth, long-fingered hands probed her neck.

"Now I'll listen to your chest."

He slid the paper kimono down over her shoulders. She heard him put on the stethoscope and waited for him to touch her. There was a long pause, and Ellen stirred.

"I'm trying to warm the disk," he explained. Ellen smiled. The disk touched her upper chest and traveled back and forth across the breastbone, resting a moment at each stop, as though on an invisible track. It continued traveling down the side of each breast and deftly slipped between them. Dr. Rostow's head was bent low, almost touching hers. She could feel the warmth of his face only inches away. He smelled good, with a natural sweetness not masked by aftershave lotions and hair tonics.

"Breathe, please," he reminded her. "Good. Again. Deeper. Hmm, sounds good. Now let me listen to your back."

The warm disk started its journey, but its course was not as predictable as before. It hopped more or less randomly along the outer portions of her rib cage. Ellen could feel him exhaling near her shoulder in warm, silent puffs.

"Breathe again. Good. Now deeply."

The disk rose and fell, each time touching softly and lingering like a kiss.

"Now you can lie down. I'd like to listen again in this position, but so far everything sounds normal."

Again the disk began to travel in unhurried circles around her breasts. Ellen relaxed with Dr. Rostow's mild pace. She felt him leaning over her, close enough to detect his warmth.

"You sound fine," he announced, straightening up. "My guess is that you experienced paroxysmal atrial tachycardia." While he went on to explain this harmless condition, Ellen felt a tear well up in one eye and trickle awkwardly toward her ear. She wondered whether it was relief or his gentleness that had moved her.

As Dr. Rostow continued through the abdominal and neurological phases of the examination, his concentration relaxed a little, and he asked her about her work.

"What do you teach?"

"English and American literature."

"Really?" he replied with interest. "You be must much better-read than I. I hardly ever read for pleasure," he admitted as he closed the paper smock over her and raised her to a sitting position. "I know I should."

"But then it wouldn't be much of a pleasure, would it?" laughed Ellen.

"True," he agreed, "but, really, I think I'd like to. Can you recommend a good book?"

Several titles immediately came to mind.

"Have you read *Angle of Repose*?" she asked.

"No. Who wrote it?"

"Wallace Stegner—he's one of my favorites." Ellen went on: "He describes the sounds and smells of places so vividly that I feel I'm actually seeing them. And he creates such believable people."

"Sounds good—maybe I will," Dr. Rostow added with a wistful sigh. Ellen wondered what else he longed to do. "You can get dressed now," he continued, "and then I'll come and bring you to my office."

"No," answered Ellen, "I can find it."

Ellen dressed quickly and noticed her heart was beating with such a strong, steady rhythm that she wondered if the arrhythmias had ever really occurred. She brushed her hair and returned to the office.

100

"Ellen, I'm writing a prescription for digoxin, which I would like you to take once a day. It should discourage these episodes."

Ellen heard but concentrated more on feeling the gentle vibrations of his voice wash over her. She wanted to glean all the information she could about him. Did diplomas line the walls along with photos of his wife and children?

Suddenly she asked, "Where did you train?"

"I went to Yale Medical School and did most of my postgraduate training at the University of California."

"Are there pictures of your family?"

"Yes, my two daughters."

"And your wife?"

"We're divorced. They live with her."

"Oh." Ellen stopped, blushing at her boldness. In her embarrassment, she began to fumble with her coat.

"Here," he said, coming to her side and helping her into her coat. "You know, I like your dress."

"Thank you."

"How do you manage to shop?"

"With a friend usually," she replied with amusement.

As he saw her to the door, he continued, "I'm a terrible dresser. Even other doctors say my clothes are tacky, so I guess I'm glad you can't see me. Isn't that a terrible thing to say?"

Ellen laughed.

"Here's your prescription. I'd like you to make an appointment to see me in six weeks."

Ellen spent the next weeks daydreaming probably more than all of her adolescent students combined. She found herself misplacing things and was impatient with her lover, Richard, who expected to monopolize her time. Ellen grew distant and secretive the more she embroidered her romantic fantasy. She rolled the name, Harvey Rostow, over and over in her mind. How well it suited his low, velvety voice. There was something vibrant, she thought, about its trochaic cadence.

Ellen constructed a patchwork quilt of wishes and memories, sensations and desires. The clever dialogues that swirled in her head sometimes made her laugh aloud. She replayed her office visit again and again, remembering the way he showed compassion and still made her feel whole and able.

In anticipation of her next appointment Ellen's daily regimen of exercises and yoga became more exciting. Because he had noticed her clothes, she shopped for something new to wear. Quite irrationally, she ended up at a small, exquisite lingerie shop, a closet of a store that always thrilled her with its exotic array of smells and sensations. Sachets hung in embroidered packets among the racks of satin and lace and flannel gowns or were hidden among the little baskets of panties and bras that lined the counters. The more expensive imports were pinned to hanging vertical panels that could be turned like pages of a huge book. Ellen's hands fluttered over the lace and ribbon trim, savoring the tiny rosettes and bows and appliquéd designs. She knew the prices would be staggering and was glad she couldn't see them; she might have spent less time adoring each piece. Finally she made her selection, a French lace bra with rosebuds on the front over the clasp and a matching bikini with rosebuds on each hip.

Ellen arrived on time for her appointment to find others crowded in the small waiting room. The air was stale in the windowless room despite the circulation from air-conditioning vents overhead. It was more than forty-five minutes before the crisp receptionist called her name and showed her to the office.

"The doctor will be right in," she chirped as she shut the door.

Ellen waited. His telephone never stopped ringing. There are probably four lead-in lines, she thought, all stranded on Hold. Impulsively, she reached out to examine the telephone and groped around the surface of the desk. She collided with a stack of thick manila folders. Next to it lay a shorter pile of large X-ray envelopes and beyond that were scattered notepapers, probably memos, and stapled glossy pages torn from journals. Ellen drew back, rebuked. She hadn't counted on his being so busy. The daydream conversations she had rehearsed with so much anticipation would have no place in a rushed office visit. Just as Ellen was wondering whether he would even remember her, she heard a door down the hall open and his crepe-soled shoes approach. He paused outside the office to pick up her folder from the rack. Some pages turned, and then the door opened.

"Hello, Ms. Rossiter, uh, oh, Ellen."

The hem of his starched lab coat brushed her knees as he swept past and flung himself into the swivel chair on the other side of his desk.

"How are you doing?" he asked routinely.

"Just fine," she answered. There was a weary edge in his voice that hadn't been there before. She went on to say that not a single episode had occurred since she had been on the medication.

"Good," he answered distractedly. She heard him writing in her chart. It suddenly struck her that she would have no further reason to see him. The very thought was enough to make her heart stop. She imagined herself swooning to the floor and his leaping to her rescue. Frantic to save her, he would lean over, pressing his lips to hers . . . .

"In that case," he continued, "I think you should stay on it another two weeks and call if these episodes recur."

"I see."

"In the meantime, I'll send a report to Dr. Lewis," he concluded wearily.

"Thank you."

Ellen heard him closing the folder.

"You sound a little down," she added.

"I do?"

"Yes, your voice seems lower and slightly hoarse. Do you have a cold?"

"No," he answered contemplatively. There was a heaviness in his legs and a throbbing at his temples—all normal this late in his day. "Maybe I'm just tired."

"Is every day this busy?"

"Usually."

"Do you mind?"

"I don't question it."

He stopped, noting that her intrusive questions did not annoy him. He realized how easy it would be to drop his professional façade with this unflinching listener, to tell her anything and know that she would be there—alert, intelligent, and receptive. Censored thoughts overwhelmed him. How much I would like to be with her, maybe just for dinner, but that would be unethical, impossible. I should send her back to Dr. Lewis, wait a proper interval, six months or a year.

"Oh, I almost forgot!" Ellen opened her purse and took out a copy of *Angle of Repose*. "This is probably a terrible time to give you this; you're probably too busy to read it."

"Why, thank you! How very nice!" He sounded genuinely pleased. "I'd love to talk with you about it. Can you come back in six weeks?"

Suddenly the absurdity of his proposal overwhelmed him. Asking a patient to return to discuss a book! Did it constitute malpractice? Would he be sued? Ostracized by his colleagues? And how would his secretary bill Blue Cross? How would he ever account for this?

"Fine," Ellen was saying as if his proposal were a logical part of his therapy. She rose and began putting on her coat. He came and held it for her. She eased into it and turned toward him. She hesitated shyly and asked: "Would you let me see your face?"

"Of course," he answered in confusion.

Then, with the accuracy of someone sighted, she raised both hands to his face and delicately swept across his brow and down along the sides of his cheeks and chin. Her fingers brushed over his lips and traced his nose and eyebrows, then retreated back to his hairline, following it down over his sideburns and past his ears. She felt the throbbing pulse in his warm neck and quickly withdrew her hands, aware of his unease. She thanked him and walked serenely to the door.

Though her exploration lasted only a few seconds, it completely violated what little was left of Dr. Rostow's sense of proper doctor-patient decorum. He became aware of a liquifying weakness in his knees and groin. He wanted to call her back, but his throat constricted so that he could not have uttered a syllable if his life depended on it. In the doorway Ellen turned to him, smiling, and said, "See you."

It's Always Summer

It's always summer when you're around
isn't that funny?
Even when it's raining outside
and we lie on our bed shivering.
Your hands are warm
your body toasts me,
your lips are warm rivers
I drift down the Mississippi.
Your skin is golden
it shines all over me.
Your eyes are rays of sunshine
that sparkle in the dark.
Your arms are branches of tall trees
that enfold me.
Green leaves and honeybees.
Buzz around me loverboy,
I need more summer.

Prince Charming

They tell me
there is no
Prince Charming.
He is a fantasy
of the unliberated
masses.
Then why do I stroke
your silky skin
with such pleasure
and caress your
lean back with
trembling fingers?
If you aren't Prince Charming
who are you?

Ann's Hood Canal Oysters

*The most sensuously delicious protein pigout I know is simple to prepare
but, like caviar, hard to come by. The dish is fresh Hood Canal oysters
that have been plucked off the beach at low tide and grilled on an open
campfire. Slurped and guzzled with white wine and sourdough French
bread, they make a soul-satisfying banquet that needs its own framework
to be perfect.*

*Your oyster feast begins with a leisurely day at one of the protected,
sand-and-rock beaches that scallop the edge of the twenty-five-mile-long
finger of the Pacific Ocean called Hood Canal in the state of Washington.
The opposing shores bathe the feet of the Olympic rain forest and mountain
range. The sky is normally moody and changeable in summer, and the air
is so different from California's that when I first arrive I feel as if I'm
enclosed in a warm, damp blanket. The air slows one's movements ever so
slightly and is forever gently caressing the skin. There is a constant activity
at the water's edge—waves lapping and splashing. The water is tepid at the
wading edges and tingling crisp where it's deep enough to swim. The
snorkler sees water gardens of infinite blue and green beauty, and the
beachcomber may glimpse herons, swallows, sea gulls, migrating geese, oysters, clams, and riffling seaweed.*

*Let a driftwood fire blaze for an hour to produce perfect, slightly flam-
ing coals. Meanwhile, collect the oysters left exposed on the sand by the
receding tide. It's as easy as picking overripe berries from a bush. Place the
oysters on a grill over the coals. As they pop open one by one, remove them
from the fire, pry them fully apart with an oyster knife, slop them with*

either Crosse and Blackwell's seafood sauce or lemon juice, and devour them. Cooked properly, they will be sweet, succulent, and slithery. Overcooked, they will resemble shoe leather. Feed such failures to the sea gulls. Indulge your own palate with nothing but perfection. When sated, build up the campfire again, sit cozily by it, toasting your front and chilling your back until the night gently enfolds and the incoming tide softly laps the world to peace.

IV. FORBIDDEN FRUIT

A few of us, especially the ones from religious backgrounds, had the opportunity to acquire a sense of sin at an early age. The ensuing war between the flesh and spirit infused sexual experience with matchless intensity and produced enough psychological fallout to taint a lifetime. The list of sins grew as fast as we did. Instead of quashing our lust, the concept of sin turned fleeting thoughts into erotic dynamite. That denial can be most arousing was borne out with the zeal in which we engaged in discussions about the forbidden. Our verbal debaucheries incited us to break lifelong taboos and to unleash censored passions in the group of stories called For-bidden Fruit. *Those of us who had the misfortune to have grown up rationally in more liberal climates sometimes yearn for that which we were denied—the exotic taste of forbidden fruit.*

The Tender and the Wanton Where They Cross

Tenderness informs the fingertips and guides the blood
Beating in the hope-scarred heart
Soothes the pertinent hand from tremors of deferred desire
Loosens the searching lips for deeper quenching
Gives the hipbones the softening glide
Strengthens the spine to hold back force
Hoarsens into deep the whispered voice
Cheers the sharing spirit on to share yet more
And gives the love-burst magnitude and flight.

Wantonness slips past the protest of the spoken No
Stammered through the starving flesh
Demands electric answers of the nerves
Tingling from skin-touch into visceral surge
Tongues the tender archways into caves
Pulling breath to gasp and gasp to moan
Thrusts the thighs and curves the back
Opens liquid flesh to deepest drive
And flashes purest lightning through the mind's dark dome.

The tender and the wanton where they cross
Fuse the hot bliss bringing reason's body home.

Schübling, Liebling:
A Bawdy Tale

A Schübling is a sausage, but definitely not a hot dog, a wiener or a frank-furter. It is fat rather than long, and it is juicy on the inside and crisply taut on the outside. To be honest, the juice is mostly fat. If you bite into a Schübling, the fat runs down your cheek and drops over your hands. This is a messy experience, sloppy and crude, but well worth losing your dignity for because it allows you to be human, to let go of your inhibitions, to smell, salivate, suck, and chew without shame.

You will, of course, hold the Schübling with your fingers—never touch it with a knife and fork. The feeling of this hot, fat piece of resilient sausage underneath its stretched-out skin, at this point still innocently dry, deter-mines whether you will go through with the experience or not. A lukewarm, limp Schübling is not worth approaching with your lips. Push it aside and reach for another. A word of caution here: any attempt to reheat a cooled-off Schübling leads to dismal failure.

Once you have satisfied your tactile sense, bend down and inhale the aroma. Is it strong and tangy? Can you sniff out the freshness of good meat? Then it is ready for intimate contact with your tongue. You may try any of these variations, depending on your mood. Are you ravenous? Then take a hearty bite and enjoy. If you like the sensation of the dry, hot surface inside your mouth, hold on to it before you let your teeth rupture the skin. Or you may take a tiny bite first, lick off just a few drops of juice at a time, alter-nating between sucking and chewing. Whatever you do at the beginning, you will be drooling in the end. Your eyes will water, your nose will run, your cheeks will glisten while you smack your lips and lick your fingers, uncon-

cerned with disapproving stares. Yes, do it in public. Schüblings are steamed in public squares and fairgrounds. Do it in front of everybody. Do it in pairs and in groups. Know that you, too, are a member of the human race.

Frau Becker stepped out onto the balcony of her brand-new Swiss chalet. She took a deep, appreciative breath of the mountain air. Once again her husband had been right when he picked this particular place. It offered every modern convenience, including a sauna next to the obligatory atomic shelter in the basement, and the view was unmolested by any trace of tourism. The ancient farmhouses clung to the steep hillside like a flock of grazing sheep protected by the shepherd, a small white church with a pointed belfry, which sat on top of the cluster as if to ward off the majestic flow of the distant glacier.

Herr Becker had bought the chalet in the winter, but now in mid-August the gleaming white caps of the mountains contrasted dramatically with the lush green slopes, while cowbells tinkled pleasantly from all directions. Frau Becker hoped that the weather would hold until September 15 when she expected friends for a weekend party. Right now the walls were bare and the rooms empty, but in four weeks' time she would fill the place with rustic furniture, dried flowers, and local color. She had done it before in Greece and Portugal. There she had given herself more time, of course. Only in Switzerland could she be sure that the workmen would arrive on schedule and that her chairs and tables would be delivered when promised.

Before Herr Becker had made so much money in real estate, Frau Becker had stretched their budget by doing a lot of things herself; they had built their first house in Stuttgart practically with their own hands—plastering, painting, hammering, and gardening. Even now, she surprised her friends with hand-crocheted afghans, hand-woven baskets, or homemade pies. In the eyes of their large circle of acquaintances, Frau Becker exemplified the German housewife of the old school who hustled and bustled all day long to keep everything clean and make everybody comfortable. Without his wife, they said, Herr Becker would never have made it because Waltraud Becker was not only industrious, or "fleissig" as they say in German, but also beautiful and charming.

She was indeed Herr Becker's "greatest asset," they would add jokingly. How sad that their only son and heir to the real estate empire had turned out so badly. As far as anyone knew, he had gone to India after doing a lot of disgusting things with his hair and body, and was never heard from again.

On August 15, exactly four weeks before her big party, Waltraud Becker had many things on her mind other than her estranged son; but in the pocket of her apron she carried a letter signed with her son's new religious name. In it he warned her to change her diet and to turn away from materialistic endeavors. As she glanced at the clear blue sky over the mountain range, she felt closer to her son than she had in all the years of his tumultuous growing up, and more than anything else she would like to have shared this moment with him. But if she had any regrets, she did not let them surface. There were many things she did not dwell on—for instance, why she no longer loved her husband. If she could do nothing about them, why brood over them?

Better to get busy with her tasks. She returned to her all-electric kitchen, picked up her ruler, and began to measure the floor for the right-sized table. Would she prefer a butcher block? She had seen a beautiful old piece in the market; maybe the butcher would sell it to her. Her deliberations absorbed her so deeply that it took some time before the noise outside entered her consciousness.

When she went to see what was going on, she could not believe her eyes. A large bulldozer was winding its way up the narrow road, followed by a crane and a truckload of workers. The procession stopped right in front of her balcony where she now discovered the square outline of a newly started building site. She knew right away that her party was ruined, that the chalet was a mistake, and that she would have to call her husband in Stuttgart immediately so that he could get his lawyers to rescind the deal. It would be futile to buy the furniture or to do anything but concentrate on abandoning the chalet and canceling the party. Cables would have to be sent; a string of actions had to be set in motion.

But Frau Becker didn't pick up the phone. Instead, she pulled up a chair to watch the proceedings at the building site. She didn't know why, because she was not a contemplative woman. Was it because she could not bring herself to get in touch with her husband, to deal with his anger, to listen to his tirade? Was it that she suddenly enjoyed the notion of receiving her guests in a house bare of furniture, next to an ugly construction site? Or was she simply tired of buying matching towels and soaps and curtains and rugs and dishes and sectional couches?

Frau Becker had always been fascinated by building sites. The machines were so much larger than the men that they seemed to do the job on their own. Steadily, they went about their business with a great sense of purpose, like well-trained animals. The crane moved its long neck gracefully from right to left picking up large crates from the truck and putting them down gently on the grass. The bulldozer dug its heavy haunches into the ground, burrowing its head deeper and deeper into the wet earth. And the cement mixer bounded and twirled around and around until a creamy thick paste poured from its narrow opening at the bottom. The men were there, of course, patting and stroking the metal bodies to make them go up or down, forward or backward. Quite obviously they knew how to handle the truck to make it tilt its back so willingly or to get the tip of the crane to plunge precisely into such a small hole. Sometimes the men themselves joined their machines, feeding their voracious mouths with big shovels of sand or loading their backs with bricks. Sometimes they switched roles and became servants where before they had been masters, lifting and carrying large pieces of wood themselves in order to place them where the machine wanted them. All day long they worked together to the same steady rhythm, embracing rocks and balancing sticks gracefully like acrobats. Men and machines, machines and men—their bodies in top condition, their movements in perfect harmony. To put one stone on top of another, to smooth out the edges with cement, to watch a house grow out of its foundations seemed to her a gratifying spectacle.

As the days went by, Frau Becker became well acquainted with everything that went on at the building site, almost as though she were part of the crew. Although she never thought of this herself, she identified with the workers like a spectator identifies with the characters of a play. Her day began at eight like theirs and ended with the first stroke of the bell at six. At noon everyone dropped his tools and went down to the Hotel Krone for lunch—everyone except one man, who ate his sandwich under a tree and then stretched out for his siesta until his comrades returned at two o'clock.

On the third day of her vigil on the balcony, Waltraud Becker decided to bake a cake. She felt that she had been sitting around too long without doing anything, particularly since the men were so busy all the time, and here she was—a lazy tourist with nothing to do. In order to get the necessary ingredients, she had to hike down to the village and buy everything, including a baking tin. Then she climbed back to her kitchen and made a chocolate cake. At noon she put the cake into a basket, together with a thermos bottle full of freshly filtered black coffee, and carried it over to the man under the tree.

The man seemed quite surprised. He put down the bread and sausage he was eating and accepted a piece of cake. In return he offered her one of his sausages—a Schübling. This local specialty was known to be especially crisp and juicy. Frau Becker declined politely, but had some cake and coffee with him. He ate two large pieces, gulping the hot coffee with appreciative slurps. They both drank straight from the bottle. Frau Becker put her mouth where his had been, and he noticed it.

"Good cake, good coffee," he said with a smile. From his accent she gathered that he was Yugoslavian. She had expected this since most construction workers in Switzerland came from Yugoslavia. And like all Yugoslavian construction workers this one was handsome, strong, clean, and courteous. She guessed his age at about thirty-five. The children in the picture he showed her were eight, ten, and twelve. His wife, with her head covered by a white kerchief, was ageless like peasant women everywhere. He would go back in two years, he said. The last time he had seen them was three years ago. Frau Becker nodded. She knew more than he imagined about Yugoslavian workers because she had seen a documentary film on television. After he had shown her the picture, he offered her a drink from his bottle of schnapps. Again, she did not wipe off the rim but licked it with her tongue. He cautiously put his hand on her ankle and, when she did not object, he moved it slowly up and under her skirt. They understood each other very well.

Next to the tree was a small ravine through which tumbled a noisy little creek. The grass felt soft, if a bit wet down there, and trees protected them from all sides. Frau Becker was not disappointed that he took her very quickly because this, too, she had expected. He entered her with short, quick thrusts, but he was in no way rough or clumsy, just fast and strong like a cloudburst after a thunderstorm. Then he collapsed on top of her, mumbling, "Frau, Frau, Frau," many times over as if in prayer. This moved her immensely, and she stroked his thick woolly hair affectionately while his semen trickled out of her onto the grass. What a nice feeling to lie there, next to a rushing creek with a warm young man on top of her. For so many years she had awakened at night, aroused from orgasmic dreams which left her frustrated, that now she really enjoyed keeping her excitement warm without wanting anything more.

But from the expression on her lover's face, she gathered that more was to come, that he had something special in mind for her. Making sure that her skirt was out of the way, he slipped one hand under her ample backside and the other into his knapsack. She felt something soft and quivering, yet taut and subtle between her legs. Startled, she discovered a Schübling in his hands, but she was too absorbed by the thrilling sensations he conveyed with this unusual tool to object to it. Quite the opposite, he was so agile with this Schübling that she found it superior to anything nature had provided. This way he could easily keep a close watch on her to adjust every turn and twist to her response. He managed to drive her wild. Occasionally, he bit a piece off from his end, eating his way to her crotch where his tongue took over until she was totally satisfied and told him to stop.

From then on Frau Becker bought a lot of groceries at the local market—she never forgot to add a Schübling or two—and every day she carried another delicacy to the building site. Sometimes there was enough left for the other workers to have a taste before they went back to their machines.

When Herr Becker arrived punctually from Stuttgart for the big party, he could not understand why his wife had never informed him about the gaping hole underneath the balcony, which by then was partially filled with concrete blocks and the monstrous steel door of the atomic shelter. After he spent hours on the telephone, Herr Becker informed his wife that he had traded their chalet for a bungalow in Ibiza and that they would leave immediately to have a look at it.

But Frau Becker refused to abandon the chalet. She applied for a job as a waitress at the Hotel Krone. The owner did not feel comfortable with a rich lady in his service, but waitresses were hard to find in such a small village, and she had agreed to work for very little. If the Krone owner had hoped that Frau Becker would bring him new and better customers from among her own people, he was disappointed. But she proved to be a good worker, the best he ever had, and she soon took over his job as cook. And the construction workers liked her cooking so much that they never went anywhere else.

Pope Innocent XV:
Scenes from a Dream

Scene I

The pope is coming! I have been invited to a banquet by the chairman of our Twentieth High School Reunion Committee. She has reserved the private banquet room at Trader Vic's. Our class is hostessing the gala event with the kind of excitement that is fueled by short notice.

Awaiting us is the dining room swaddled lavishly in gold and white crepe de chine, a perfect camouflage for His Holiness. I approach the long white table that stretches like a satin freeway into the far reaches of an adjoining room. The brilliance of each place setting stuns me. Not only is the cutlery of pure gold, but each plate and goblet is of an original design that exactly conveys the individuality of each special guest. As I look among the place settings anxiously seeking my own, I realize that they are the work of Judy Chicago. The item expressing the unique essence of each receiver is the goblet. Starting first with the simplest, they become increasingly elaborate and ornate. The smooth, gentle lines and creamy glazes of the early goblets do not prepare me for the drama of the later ones. Great convoluted lips seethe with textured glazes and laugh defiantly at the limitations of their porcelain. One of these bold vessels draws me to it and swallows my will. I wonder how I will ever drink from its frothy folds. As I take my seat, I realize too late that this garish goblet is not meant for me. I look up alarmed and meet the amused glance of the pope, who is seated directly across from me.

Poise. I am summoning every ounce of poise while I smile back and plot a gracious retreat. Just then another truth assaults me: all my female classmates are wearing hats. Proper black hats. Some are velvet, some have veils, but all are exactly right. I know I have forgotten mine. The thought had not even occurred to me. My hand rises tentatively to my head to confirm my fear. I pray for a hat. I touch my head, and to my amazement there is a hat! Relief overwhelms me until I look up and see that my hat is not like anybody else's. It is a sailor's hat, dirty and battered, with its rim yanked down over my eyes. Panic returns.

I scan the room. I see my Jewish friends. They are bareheaded too, and they are being seated in the adjoining room where scurrying waiters are still setting the table. I eagerly rise and join them, glad to have found my rightful place.

The dinner is about to begin. Someone at my end of the table has just shot a roll of film processing our arrival. She frees the cartridge from the camera and pulls out some already processed footage. We greedily examine the tiny still frames, searching for ourselves. The camera is a novelty. It photographs people's underwear. I look more closely at the transparent figures on the ribbon of film.

The other women wear exquisite lingerie. They have not been caught short. I see lovely bikinis, a few garter belts with stockings, and even an occasional black, strapless Merry Widow. I hadn't known they were back in vogue. But now I see a figure different from the rest. She is naked. I see the nipples, the pubic hair, and, most conspicuously, the ribs. It is me. The pope looks at me. He likes me—no, he wants me. Of all the women in the room he has chosen me. I am the chosen one. He indicates that he will come to my house.

Scene II

I am home again in my sunny kitchen. I want to start dinner, but the pope is standing in the way. His elaborate gowns cascade in brocade layers and fill the entire space between the stove and sink and the counter opposite. He seems not to notice my noisy children in their filthy cutoffs cavorting in the surf of his outer garments. I am angry with them for being no more ready for this distinguished occasion than

I am. I want to reprimand them, but first I should introduce them, and I don't know how. Does the pope have a title? Your Majesty or Your Highness? No, those are too regal. Your Excellency? No, too secular. What about Sir? No, too short. Is his last name O'Neill? Mr. O'Neill? No, that doesn't sound right.

The pope is gesturing toward the dishwasher. He has never seen one before and wants me to show him how to use it. I try to teach him how to load it, but he is incapacitated by his stiff gowns and can't get quite close enough to place the dishes in their appropriate slots. Each time he bends over, his huge pointed hat threatens to fall into the sink.

He is distracted by my Princess wall phone. He has never seen one and eagerly glides over to examine it. While he is trying to place a call in Polish to the Vatican, my husband rushes in wearing sweaty tennis gear. He is not ready either, and I still haven't started dinner. I am getting frantic. I gesture to my husband, "How shall we introduce him?"

My husband finds a small piece of scrap paper and writes: "YOUR DELIVERANCE."

The pope floats back into the kitchen. Tactfully my husband withdraws. The pope is used to people withdrawing tactfully. He raises his hand majestically. I stand rapt. Slowly he begins to twirl, gradually gaining momentum so that his gowns begin to lift. I see his immaculate slippers, then his black silken stockings fasted below the knee with maroon garters. He spins faster. The robes rise above his strong, chunky thighs, and I behold him—in Excelsis Deo! He *is* Omnipotent, Infallible.

There is not enough room in the kitchen, so I lead him to the living room where the ladies are waiting. They are kneeling in parallel rows, black-laced Christians in one, naked Jewesses in another. Again he nods to me. I am to remove his garments. Carefully I expose the priceless layers, draping each one over my velvet couch, over the chairs, the desk, the coffee table. Revealed at last, the pope reclines contentedly on my deep pile carpet. His glorious erection points heavenward.

One by one we take turns paying obeisance to it. The most devout kneel before it, awed. Others beg favors in low, beseeching voices. Some mount it and glide dreamily up and down like glassy-eyed children on a carousel. When my guests are finished, I lower myself over the pope. I come instantly, again and again, electrified by his blessing. The pope winks at me smugly, then closes his eyes and murmurs: "Amen." Our audience is over. Obediently we file out, leaving him erect and glowing, the everlasting light.

Feliny (sic)

Fingers splayed, I slide my hand
through the thick furry vulnerability
of her belly.
Her legs drop open, wantonly,
and she stretches her neck,
sinking her head into the tightly whiskered carpet,
waiting for my fingers to reach
her silken neckpieces.

From ear to breastbone to groin
I trace five sharpened fingernails,
lingering to press the heel of my hand
into the soft hollowed expanse
between her legs, watching intently as her eyes
become glinting slits of pleasure
and her mouth quivers slightly open
as if to whisper to me in feline tongue.

Her breath is warm and sweet
as I lower my face to hers.
My fingers explore her jellied flesh
with slow insistence, and my rings gleam through her long
black fur as I circle the trembling
moistened spot we now share.

Her tail swishes in sudden violence
and she raises her tiny head,
staring at me through enigmatic eyes,
wary, speechless.
"Hello," I purr.

Trio

"What a beautiful woman," people said after meeting Marsha. The strand of silver in her long mane of auburn hair had nothing to do with age. Age had nothing to do with Marsha. Marsha was an island. Once you set foot there, you entered her territory. You accepted her age, her language, her smell, her scenery. Bewitched, you forgot where you came from.

John was no exception. When I had invited Marsha to spend the summer with us at our cabin on the lake, I knew this might happen. Marsha had always preferred artistic men—painters, poets, actors, men who made a fuss over her, lured by her composure, her mysterious stillness, which they took for strength. But like a mountain pool that draws its water from invisible springs, Marsha nourished her outward calm from constant turmoil deep within herself. Inevitably, she attracted restless souls, who deceived themselves about her and drowned.

Yet John was anything but a restless soul. He was the solid rock in our ten-year marriage. Before I had met him, my life had been very much like Marsha's: a divorce, a series of jobs and relationships, and a lot of madcap schemes about saving enough money to start a gallery in Boston or in London or on the West Coast. Meanwhile, Marsha had made a name for herself as a landscape architect, and I had married John and ventured into motherhood at the ripe age of thirty-five. John taught math, and every summer we added another room to our cabin at the lake to house hordes of boys including John's two sons from his first marriage.

Of course he would go for Marsha, who was so different from me, so detached, so alluringly passive. I watched his mating dance at first with amusement: his furtive glances, his intense conversations with her about casual matters, the sudden self-revelations. At night, the three of us drank a lot and swam in the moonlight without bathing suits. Afterward John and I made love. It was like starting all over again. We had both become different around Marsha, more alive, more sexy, competing for her attention. Even the boys faded into the background. When they finally left for camp, we hardly noticed their absence. It seemed strange to me how John and Marsha avoided being alone. As soon as I disappeared into the kitchen, they trailed after me offering to help. When I went shopping, they piled into the car with me. Then when John wanted us all to drive to San Francisco together, I changed the game. "Nothing will take me away from the lake," I said to Marsha. "You go with John; you haven't been to San Francisco for years." They didn't put up too much resistance; it was as if they had been waiting for my signal. So off they went.

I felt no jealousy; at least I did not recognize my own involvement in their affair as jealousy. Quite the opposite—I felt intoxicated with power. Even while they were gone, I felt elated. I saw myself in the golden glow of a magnanimous giver. I dreamed up visions of two caressing bodies on a secluded beach at Fort Cronkite or in a Victorian four-poster. Sometimes I was Marsha, sometimes I was John. Slowly he pulled back her nightgown. I saw her naked, her hair spread over the pillow like Snow White. I watched John kneel down and kiss her forehead, gently, reverently, shyly even. Her small breasts greeted his first touch. But her long, nimble thighs stayed close together. Virginal. Ophelia. Still kneeling, he sucked her nipples; they were not virginal but experienced, gourmet nipples, now encouraging to proceed down toward the auburn bush of Irish heather growing from her crotch. For the first time he smelled her woman perfume—Irish heather, Irish moss—that exhilarating perfume of a woman waiting to be tasted, yearning to open her thighs.

Marsha takes her time—a mountain lake that won't warm up until it has soaked up the summer sun. John's hands are summer sun. They

126

singe through ice. They are patient because, in the end, they will win. Languidly, she allows him to penetrate the mossy crevices guarding her privacy even in the most intimate embrace. His lips take over from his hands until she opens herself completely to him. Even at the point of climax, she clenches her fists, fighting to keep to herself. They look at each other like adversaries in the heat of battle. For a moment her green eyes stare at him wide open, broken with ecstasy. Over and over he plunges into the mountain pool, which is no longer calm.

My tension mounted as the day came to an end. I found myself listening for the car, anticipating their return. What if they didn't come back? Watching the golden cast of the evening sun over the lake, I thought of the Greek tyrant Polycrates, who threw his most precious ring into the ocean as a gift to the gods. A fish was brought to him and inside it was the ring. The gods had refused his bribe. They took his wife, his children, his castle, and his kingdom too.

Had I tossed my wedding ring into the water? Was I tempting fate with my little game? It never occurred to me that it was their game until I heard voices downstairs. They did not call me. They had started a life without me.

When John came to bed, I pretended to be fast asleep, but I was jumpy as a cat on the prowl. He took his time brushing his teeth and going through his regular routine. Finally, he turned off the light and slipped under the covers. His arms reached around my waist. His body felt warm and familiar pressed to my own as if it belonged nowhere else. I nestled against him.

"I love you," he murmured as if he had heard my silent question. Cupping his hands around my breasts, he began to stroke my backside with his swollen penis. In his embrace, my excitement returned. I could not forget that he had been with Marsha. I kept seeing her stretched out under him, longing for him, waiting to be touched by him. When he entered me, I was her, and my vagina throbbed greedily against his cock. It is touching me where it has touched her, I thought, and suddenly the electric charge of an orgasm jolted my body into knowing what I really wanted.

As usual, John went promptly to sleep. I cautiously extracted myself from his tight embrace. He continued to breathe deeply. A slightly smug expression lingered on his face.

Marsha's door was unlocked. She sat huddled in bed with a book on her knees. Her hair covered her like a tent. She looked up apprehensively: "Is something wrong?"

"No, everything is just right," I answered. Gently I eased her back on the bed, spreading her hair over the pillow. I sat down beside her and kissed her forehead. Slowly I pulled back her nightgown. She was snow white. She did not resist.

Voyeuses

The waitress leaned over to wipe the table, and Janet caught a glimpse inside her shirt, provocatively and deliberately unbuttoned. She caught the curve of her young breast down to the nipple before the young woman straightened up.

"Would you like a menu?" she asked brightly.

"No," Janet answered. "Just coffee, please."

Janet looked around the café. A young couple were holding hands at a table in front of a large picture window; they were clearly oblivious to the sun-speckled ocean outside. The man was a little husky with shoulder-length dark hair and rather large features that strained to be handsome. The girl was petite, full-bodied, with thick, wavy, dark hair that she repeatedly pushed back over her shoulders, revealing her bare, tanned skin and full breasts oozing up from a tight elasticized bandeau that compressed what some men would have called "a great pair of eyes." Janet winced to hear herself think that, for she hated the expression but couldn't explain why. A man in his thirties, dressed in working clothes—a mechanic?—looked at the couple from time to time and smoked a cigarette down to toke size before jamming it out in his saucer. A casually but impeccably dressed older woman was seated at the counter. She swiveled her stool around slightly, but Janet couldn't tell whether she was staring out at the ocean or at the couple or both.

No one else came into the café, and, slowly, they all began to form a strange, silent community for Janet. As she looked at the scene in front of her, it was as if a director had said: "Places everyone!" before the curtain call. The waitress brought her coffee and a check and walked away. The young man laughed softly and kissed his girlfriend on the nose. The girl smiled, almost shyly, and Janet noticed that for all her voluptuousness—clearly appreciated by the devouring eyes of her friend—there was a sweet innocence about her.

Janet reached into her bag, pulled out the hard-covered journal she always carried with her, and thumbed past scribblings, sketches, and half-finished stories to find a clean page. Without thinking, she placed her left arm across the book so that only a minimum amount of writing space was visible to any would-be onlooker. That no one was in a position to look over her shoulder was a thought Janet did not consider; the gesture was automatic. She stared at the young couple for a second and then watched the blue ink flow as she started to write:

"The Café"

Janet hesitated. She looked at the couple again and saw him move his face close and say something. Janet couldn't hear him. She looked down at her journal and started to write again:

"You know what I want to do right now is take you out on the beach and fuck you."

"Oh Gary!" The girl looked away with a smile on her face that betrayed her mock protest.

"What's the matter? We're not exactly strangers, you and I," he teased.

"But after last night, Gary? Really!"

"Hey, I'm not one of those old farts who needs a week to recover! Whaddya think?" Gary looked hard at her for a minute, and then said:

"Listen, I just can't get enough of you. You are one hot piece."

"Gary, please don't talk like that. You make me feel cheap." The girl looked down at her hands, and the smile vanished. Gary's face clouded, and he put his fingers under her chin, raising her face to his.

"Baby, hey . . . I'm sorry. I didn't mean it that way. I just mean . . . oh hell, you know what I mean."

She was obviously soothed by his sudden contriteness and answered softly: "It's okay." And then: "You are a classy lover, I've got to give you that." She smiled again, as though surprised by her own words or the admission of her feelings. Gary's face brightened.

"Come on, sweetheart. There's not a soul out there. Let's find a little spot. I've got a blanket in the trunk. I can make you real happy. You know that." He stroked her cheek.

"Yeah," she answered. "You sure can." They giggled, and he pressed his face into her thick mane of soft hair.

"Whaddya say? Let's split, okay?"

"Okay," she said, "but I don't want nobody around, you promise?"

"I promise, I promise," Gary said, jumping up quickly and taking her by the hand. She was slow to get up, and Gary tugged at her. He left money on the table and, as they pushed their way out of the swinging door, the eyes of the other customers followed them. A young mechanic, alone at a small table, jammed out a cigarette into his saucer and left on their heels; a woman in her late thirties stopped writing in her notebook; and another woman, probably in her fifties, looked up from her stool at the counter, her face expressionless.

The two women remaining looked at each other, the younger one in jeans and a thick navy sweater, her hair tied back in a ponytail; the other dressed in a casual but expensive pants suit, the then fashionable safari-olive color, with a bright red scarf tied around her gray-blonde hair. The younger of the two wore no makeup and had the healthy look of someone who was comfortable with herself yet derived satisfaction from doing rather than being. The older woman looked like someone whose monied way of life had frozen her at an indeterminate age for years to come. Her face was expertly made-up; only a woman would know how long it took to achieve the effect of ageless insouciance.

As if on cue, they got up at the same moment and waited beside each other for the waitress to take their money. The writer left first. On impulse, she didn't go to her car but, instead, crossed the street to the beach. It was quiet but not yet hot enough for beachgoers, and anyway, it was a notoriously windy spot. She stopped to pull off her tennis shoes and then dug her toes into the sand. Stringing her shoes together by their laces, she flung them over her shoulder and began to walk. Ahead of her at some distance, she saw the couple from the café. They were walking hand in hand. Occasion-

ally, they stopped to kiss each other, but the girl always wriggled free, running ahead and making him chase her.

Not wanting to intrude on them, the woman dallied. She stopped to look at the water, her hands on her hips, her head thrown back. From the corner of her eye, she caught sight of a figure on the beach and turned to look. It was her companion from the café. If she seemed out of place at the café, perched on a stool (and she had, *the writer thought), she seemed even more incongruous on the beach, her sandals in her hand, her leather pouch over her arm. The younger woman turned away from her and resumed her walk in the direction of the couple, who had disappeared from view.*

She saw some rocks in the distance that seemed like a good lookout spot and a perfect stopping place. (Doers need destinations, she mused—"be-ers" just walk aimlessly.) When the rocks were in clear view, she began to cut across the sand. At the base of the rocky mound, she sat down and put her shoes back on again. She saw the older woman following in her direction. She started up the rocks, an easy climb, to a flat area at the top. Once there, she stood for a moment to breathe in the salt air. Then she sat down, pulled off the heavy sweater, and hugged her knees to her chest. She closed her eyes and let the sun play on her face.

Suddenly, she heard low voices drifting up from below. "Gary, not so fast!" The voice was plaintive and teasing at the same time. She heard a giggle. Her heart raced. She felt like a child, caught in the delirium of being in a situation she knew was not meant for her eyes. She heard a noise from behind her and turned quickly, as if caught doing something inexplicably naughty. The older woman was making her way up the rocks. Their eyes met, and, involuntarily, she put her finger to her lips, motioning the intruder to be quiet, pointing ostentatiously down to where the couple were. With a knowing nod, the woman continued to climb.

The writer slid herself over to the next rock to make room for her companion and peered over the edge. There they were, in plain view, their blanket spread out in a small cove obscured from the rest of the beach. The girl's skimpy bandeau was curled up at her waist, and her breasts were exposed in all their fullness—breasts that before too many sunsets would fall helplessly to their sides, but which now seemed to reach up and out to the sun and to her lover's eager mouth.

She glanced behind her. Her friend was at the top now, and she motioned for her to sit down beside her, again gesturing her to be quiet. In a second, the older woman had stretched herself out gracefully on the adjoining rock. Their view could not have been better had the scene been staged.

Gary's face was buried between the girl's breasts, and his large hands cupped their fullness on each side. He raised his head and then pressed his mouth to her breast; his head bobbed gently up and down as he sucked on her nipple. Her face was to the side, and she was breathing excitedly. Gary slipped his hand down to her waist and deftly unzipped her jeans. The girl stirred and then moved her own hands down to her hips, arching her back and raising her pelvis to push the jeans the rest of the way. Gary sprang up to yank them off her feet, and the women pulled their heads back quickly, lest they be noticed. They gave each other a conspiratorial look before cautiously returning to their vigil. Gary had taken off his own jeans now and was on top of her. His ass was milky white and surprisingly small in contrast to the broad muscular back that now obscured her magnificent breasts. She pushed her hands against him, again saying, with more vehemence this time: "Gary, not so fast . . ."

He rolled off her and lay motionless on his back, breathing heavily. His stiff penis made twitching movements, as if startled by the shock of sunshine and air. She leaned over him and began to trace a childishly nail-bitten finger in slow circles around the silken, slippery head.

The two women shifted their positions on the rock and looked at each other again. The older woman smiled, and the writer smiled back, rolling her eyes playfully. They started to laugh at the same moment, and each covered her mouth to stifle the sound before it burst out. They looked down once more.

The girl giggled. "Funny, eh?" Gary said in a playful but strained voice. In a sudden motion, she went down on him, her lovely thick hair cascading over his pelvis, her warm breasts burning their way through his skin. In a sudden motion, he pulled her head away and said: "Look, baby. You want slow, that's not the way to get it."

"You do me," she said, in that same shy voice that was at odds with her full and ready woman's body. She lay back down as he raised himself up again. He took hold of the bandeau that still circled her waist and slowly rolled it past her belly to her thighs, where it imprisoned her legs like an oversized ponytail band. Then he sank his head into her crotch. His head moved in butterfly motions as his tongue darted in and around her pungent pink folds. She began to squirm and toss her head from side to side, arching her body up to his mouth. She was breathing heavily, her eyes shut tight. She entwined her hands in his hair and pulled his head closer to her, talking to herself and to him in an audible whisper.

"Oh, do it, baby, do it. Eat it. Oh God. Oh my God. Don't stop. Oh Jesus, God."

Her hand moved to her mouth and she sunk her teeth into her forefinger. He stopped suddenly and looked up at her, then yanked the bandeau from her, opened her legs, and moved inside her—all in one swift movement. The look on his face was exultant as she cried out and encircled her legs around his back. After a quick, gasping finish, he rolled off her body and lay still beside her. She was also motionless, her legs splayed, her arms limp, her head turned away from him.

The women looked at each other, their faces now close enough that each could detect light beads of perspiration on the other's skin. The writer signaled that she was going down, and the older woman nodded. They raised themselves up carefully and quietly made their way to the bottom. They walked side by side without speaking.

After some distance, the older woman turned and said, "Well!" in a bright voice. They laughed together. "I don't know about you, but I could stand a drink," the older woman said. "Yes," her friend laughed.

"I don't live far from here. Why don't you just follow me in your car? I feel I know you already. My name is Dora. What is yours?"

"I'm Denny." The two women stood solemnly on the beach and shook hands.

Janet looked up from her notebook. The older woman was smoking a cigarette and staring out the window at the ocean. Janet sipped her coffee and returned to her story.

Dora's house was an enormous mansion around the bend and up a hill from the café. Hidden in the trees, it suddenly loomed up at the end of a long driveway. Denny pulled her car in next to Dora's. As they walked to the door, Denny commented on the house.

"What a splendid place to live!"

"Yes, I love this old house," Dora answered.

"Have you lived here a long time?"

"Yes. Ever since we first married, and that was many years ago."

"Oh, is your husband likely to be here?"

"No, he died two months ago." Dora's face looked strained.

"I am sorry," Denny answered.

"Yes," Dora answered, "I'm not accustomed to it yet. I still expect to see him every time I put my key in the lock."

"Then you live alone now?" Denny said.

"Yes. It's just me and Lady. That's our dog . . . his dog, really. I'm afraid she hasn't adjusted yet either."

"Was it sudden?" Denny asked, not wanting to be one of those people who changed the subject when death is mentioned.

"Yes. It was sudden," Dora said simply, as she turned the key in the lock and beckoned Denny inside.

Dora led her through a massive dining room to the kitchen in the back of the house. It was a very large kitchen with a long refectory table in the center. Dora signaled her to sit down and strode over to the refrigerator. In a second she was back with a pitcher of martinis and two glasses.

"Why, they're all made! You must have been expecting me," Denny said brightly. Dora laughed. "Where is Lady? Doesn't she come to greet you?"

"Not lately. She sits most of the day, sulking by Dan's chair. She won't give up her vigil." Denny wasn't sure what to say next. There was a peacefulness that issued from the house and from this strange woman.

Dora was pouring the martinis in their glasses when she suddenly stopped. "Would you mind if I were to get out of these clothes? I feel constricted."

"Of course not," Denny said. Dora paused a second and her tone brightened.

"Look, I have a wonderful hot tub in my bathroom, and a soak would be just perfect now, wouldn't it?" Denny looked back at her and thought, yes, a tub would be wonderful. They quickly poured the martinis back into the pitcher and returned it to the refrigerator. Denny followed Dora up the wide staircase, through the bedroom, and into a startlingly spacious bathroom. As Denny was looking in delight at the sunken tile tub with art deco motifs around the rim, the marble sink, the thick, black fur rug, Dora called to her.

"The hot tub is in here."

Dora explained that the circular alcove housing the tub was actually an old tower cornerstone of the building. Narrow panes of stained glass had been set high into the stone walls encircling the tub area. Denny looked up. "It's like being in church," she said.

"Yes," Dora answered.

"Is there anything above?"

"Yes, we have a guest bedroom at the top of the tower. Go ahead and take off your things while I get some towels."

Denny began to take off her clothes as Dora moved over to a tall closet, almost hidden in the wall, and pulled out two thick black towels and two white terry robes.

"I can't believe today," Denny exclaimed. "I think I've fallen into some kind of wonderland."

Dora laughed. "Dan used to call me his 'Alice in Wonderland.' My hair was long and golden when we first married." She hung the robes on two python snakes posing as hooks and placed the towels on a curved bench by the tub. Dora disappeared into the bedroom. Denny finished undressing and quickly lowered herself into the water. Dora was walking back toward her now, completely naked. What a wonderful body, Denny thought; she displays it without a shred of self-consciousness. Dora had replaced the scarf around her head with a wide headband that held her hair away from her face and accentuated her delicate facial features and large blue eyes.

"I'm sorry you're already submerged," Dora said, as she lowered herself into the steaming water. "I'm in a terribly voyeuristic mood today. Anyway, I find women's bodies fascinating, don't you?"

Denny laughed. "Yes, I found myself completely entranced with that girl's body. You know, I've never watched anyone make love before. Have you?"

Dora smiled and said nothing.

"It looks as though this wasn't your first time," Denny said when no words came from Dora.

"No, this was not my first time," Dora said, extending her arms out along the rim of the tub.

How gracefully she moves, Denny thought. "Then you've done a lot of voyeuring?" Denny smiled at her made-up word and pretended not to be as surprised as she was at Dora's response.

"Yes, I have done a lot of 'voyeuring,'" Dora acknowledged her word with a warm smile. Her face suddenly became serious, and she spoke without looking at Denny.

"I loved Dan, and when I first found out he was having other women, I was terribly upset. Terribly." Dora's eyes filled with tears. "We talked about it, of course. I really did feel that I should be enough for him even after all our years together. In fact, our sex life had never been better," she said, looking at Denny again. "I hated the cliché of the situation, and the notion that men have an insatiable lust for someone new, different. I suppose that's why I did it—to transcend the cliché." Dora was quiet again, and Denny's mind was racing ahead. Did what? she yearned to blurt out but waited for Dora, who was again staring at nothing in front of her.

After a few seconds, Dora looked at her and said: "I've left you hanging there, haven't I? I don't mean to be a tease. It's just that I've not told anyone this story, and telling it is like reliving it." Dora sighed and stretched her body the length of the tub until her toes hit the opposite side by Denny's head. Denny also stretched out until her own feet were next to Dora's head.

"Well, Dan didn't do anything foolish like promise me he'd never do it again. It was soap opera enough without that. He said a lot of things—not defensively, though. He wanted me to know that it had nothing to do with me or his love, even lust, for me. It was difficult for me to hear him out. I was afraid that at any minute he would say something I couldn't bear—

something trite and inexcusable." She paused. "I used to lie awake nights thinking about the right thing to do. Through all of that, we continued to make love, and Dan was as sweet, loving, and powerful as ever. The thought of leaving him in a fit of pride, or pique, or whatever, just seemed too . . . stupid and, again, a cliché. Finally, I decided on a course of action, for I had to act. I could not do nothing. 'Bring them here, Dan,' I whispered to him one night after we had made love. He was obviously taken aback but tried not to show it. 'Bring them here?' he repeated.

"'Yes,' I said. 'Let me renovate one of the guest rooms, make it something very special—an exquisitely romantic storybook world for you and your lady loves.' 'And what will you get from that, my Alice?' he had said. 'I will watch you together with them,' I answered. Dan didn't answer right away. Then he asked if that would hurt me or if it really would give me pleasure. I wasn't sure myself when I answered him, but I was able to convince him that it would give me extraordinary pleasure, and so he agreed.

"How I worked on that room! Dan left it all to me. I wanted to have it finished quickly before I could think about what I was doing. The next day would not have been too soon. Fortunately, we have money, and I have a whole crew of people I call on whenever I want something done. The next morning, after he had left the house, I started telephoning. I selected the tower room, right above us. 'Rapunzel's Tower,' I used to call it. I had the carpenters construct an inner circle of wall within the tower so that there was a circular walkway around the room. The windows start up high, just as in this room, and I had them fitted with two-way mirror glass. Everything in the room itself is circular—the bed, the rug, the tables. It was all done in rose tones. I had speakers installed, and before each lover arrived, I would put on music—Indian flute music, sitar, that sort of thing. It's extraordinarily sensual. I put a collection of body oils and incense on one of the tables. I even designed a 'sex chair'—the perfect height and width, with a railing to hold on to."

Dora's face was radiant as she described other details of the room.

"When I had finished it down to the last detail, I brought Dan up to see it. I had turned on the music so that it would be playing when we walked into the room. I could tell from his face that he approved. He looked

at everything intently while I stood quietly watching him. He turned to me finally and said, 'I want it to be ours first.'

"He began to undress me very tenderly while I simply stood there. Then I undressed him. We stood there, naked, and just looked at each other for what seemed a long time. He enveloped me with his eyes, feasting on my body as I feasted on his. He stared fixedly at my breasts.

"We stood there, not touching, not speaking. I began to tremble and thought for a second I would come to orgasm. Finally, he pulled me toward him and carried me to the bed. He reached for one of the oils and began to rub my body with its slippery scent, slowly, sensuously, letting his hand linger on my breasts and between my legs. He stroked and caressed me like that for a long time—it seemed an eternity, and, to my surprise, I started to cry." She paused a second. "Then he moved into me, very, very slowly, and simply waited there, quite still, as he buried his head in my neck and did exquisite things with his tongue and mouth. I felt myself losing control and struggling to hold on to the moment. I knew if I moved, even slightly, this delicious agony would end."

Dora was quiet. "I'll never forget that night," she said, and closed her eyes. Her face was the face of a woman who had been gloriously fucked.

Denny waited a few seconds and then asked softly: "What about the others?"

Dora smiled without opening her eyes. Then she shifted her body in the water, sending ripples of warmth over Denny's flesh. Dora looked at her friend again.

"The first was Annette," she said. "I liked Annette. Not a beauty, really, but she was exotic in some way. Her skin was olive-toned, and her eyes were jet dark. She had extremely short black hair, almost mannish. Her mouth was very wide and full. She was taller than Dan. She had slim boyish hips and thin arms and legs, but her breasts were low and full, and the dark coloration of her nipples spread across her breasts like bruises. She used to play games with Dan in bed. Usually, she would pretend to be a cat, growling, purring, scratching at him, then sinking her teeth into his neck and laughing wildly. Dan would just lie there and let her play. She was always on top, and it was she who did the fucking. Oh how she would scream when she came!" Dora threw her head back and laughed wildly.

"How many were there?" Denny asked softly.

"Oh, many, many," Dora answered, sitting up again in the tub. "Each one is a story. The least interesting was Grace—but then, anyone with the name Grace has got to be dull as dishwater, don't you think?"

"Did Dan tell you their names?"

"Oh no. I named them myself. Grace was named Grace because she was so Grace-like." Denny bellowed, and Dora continued.

"Oh, Grace was over in a minute. She would just lie there, preening and posturing. I think Dan was determined to find a real person there, but poor Grace never did come through. I think she fancied herself in some porno flick. She always seemed to be looking for the camera."

The two women laughed.

"I don't know about you, but I'm ready for that drink," Dora said.

They climbed out of the tub and began drying themselves as they walked to the dressing room. Dora put on one of the robes and handed Denny the other. "There are some scuffs on that shelf," she said.

Once again, Denny padded dutifully back to the kitchen following this intriguing woman. Dora paused at the refrigerator door and said: "Maybe we should cool down a bit first. Let's sit out on the verandah." She led her outside to a long porch that ran the width of the house and looked out to the rocks and the sea beyond. There was a slight chill in the air now, and the sun was beginning to fade. Denny wrapped the terrycloth robe around her legs and stretched out on the chaise beside Dora.

"Wasn't it painful to watch him with those women?"

Dora looked at her sharply before answering.

"It was unbearable."

Although Denny couldn't imagine any woman being able to do what Dora had done with the degree of equanimity, Dora affected, nevertheless, she was surprised at her sudden admission and paused before speaking again.

"How long did this go on, then?"

"Right up until he died."

Dora's eyes clouded and she looked pensively at the ocean. Emboldened by Dora's obvious willingness to answer her every question, Denny continued.

"How did *he die?*" she asked.

Dora got up abruptly and disappeared into the kitchen. Denny remained where she was, confused and feeling chastened for her bluntness. Suddenly, Dora reappeared carrying the martini pitcher and two glasses on a tray, which she carefully placed on the table between them.

"I brought both olives and onions. I forgot to ask which you preferred."

Denny pierced an olive with a bright red toothpick, dipped it into her drink, and rolled it over her tongue before pulling it off its skewer and into her mouth. Dora poured herself a drink, then settled back in her chaise. "Are you warm enough?" *she said abruptly.*

"Yes, I'm fine, thank you."

"I killed him," *Dora said, and took a sip of her drink.*

Denny's head spun toward her as though she had been struck. Except for a gentle sadness that played around her eyes, Dora was perfectly composed. There was a sudden cawing of a gull overhead, and Denny thought she heard a twig break under the scampering foot of some small creature in the dunes beyond the porch.

"Oh, I tried other things first," *Dora said, breaking the silence between them.* "I got the idea of taking another woman up there with me. I had never had a sexual experience with a woman, and because the idea frightened me, I thought surely it would affect Dan. What I wanted from him, I don't really know. I suppose it was too late even then."

"And did you—find a woman?" *Denny asked.*

"Oh yes." *Dora sipped her martini and reached for another olive.* "Yes, indeed," *she said again.* "Dan was so intrigued by her, or the sight of us together, perhaps, that he asked me to invite her back for him. I felt lost, defeated. She wouldn't have done it, anyway. I knew that. Nor would I have asked her. It was then I knew what I had to do."

She was quiet again. When she looked up finally, she said: "It's quite remarkable how easy it is to kill someone. Oh, I supposed it helped that we have money, that we live in isolation, that we have few friends. The poison was easy to obtain, and our charming nineteenth-century ritual of tea at four just made it all much simpler than I suppose it would be for someone less fortunate. Imagine working all day and then having to shop, clean the house, get the children off to bed, and, somehow, in all of

141

that, manage to slip your husband some poison?" She looked concerned at the thought and sat quietly while Denny's mind careened around like a Ferris wheel gone amok.

It was decidedly chilly now, and the sun was setting in the sky. Denny looked at her watch and leaped from the chair. "I must go," she blurted out. "I've almost forgotten I had another life." Dora stood up and said: "Yes. I'm sorry, I would enjoy talking with you again and showing you Rapunzel's Tower."

Denny heard herself saying, "Yes, I would love to" as though they were dear friends arranging a lunch date. She raced back to the bathroom where her clothes hung in the little dressing area. She forced her mind to be still as she hung the robe back on its hook and jammed her legs into her underpants and jeans. She pulled a brush out of her bag and ran it through her damp hair. She felt a sense of enormous urgency and left her hair loose instead of recapturing it in a ponytail. Dora walked Denny to her car and reminded her of how to return to the highway. With a final wave, Denny pulled away and headed back to the café.

Janet looked up, her pen poised. "Weak ending," she said to herself. Her eyes scanned the café again. Only she and the older woman remained. The sun was setting. She pushed her journal back into her bag, picked up her check, and went to the counter just as the older woman approached with her check. They smiled at each other. As they waited for the waitress, the older woman spoke.

"You were writing furiously," she said. "I've never seen such total concentration."

"Yes," Janet laughed. "I was writing a story that became very absorbing. I'm afraid my characters ran away with me."

"I'm a writer, too," the woman offered. "Gothic novels." She laughed. Janet looked at her curiously. The waitress appeared, and she paid her check. It seemed impolite to say good-bye in the midst of this unfinished conversation, and so Janet waited while the other woman paid her check. They left together and walked toward the parking lot.

"I'm so isolated from other writers these days—from anyone, in fact," the woman said. "Do you come here very often?" Before Janet could answer, she continued. "I need to come out of my cocoon. Perhaps we could meet for coffee and share our writings." Her look was open and direct, and Janet perceived that she was a woman unused to being refused.

"Of course," Janet stammered. "Yes, yes, that would be pleasant." Janet had reached her car, and the woman handed her a card. Janet glanced at it.

Dora Cartright, Woods Way Lane

Janet looked up quizzically at the woman's face.

"Call me . . . anytime," Dora said. "I'm usually free at a moment's notice."

Janet paused before asking, "Do you have a dog named Lady?"

Dora laughed. "I have a dog—yes—but his name is Max. Why do you ask?"

Janet slid into the driver's seat and smiled. "I don't know. Writers are a little crazy, I guess."

"Yes," Dora laughed. "Call me."

Janet nodded and backed the car out of its white-lined slot. "Say," Dora was waving at her. "What is your name?"

"Denise—Denny," Janet answered. "Denny Mencken."

Janet waved, pushed her foot down hard on the accelerator, and sped down the highway to reality.

Just Desserts

They weren't in the habit of talking much—a fact that hadn't bothered Lilah before. Jed's physical presence alone had been enough to engage her. He was a large, big-boned man whose lumbering gait and relaxed slouch always reminded her of a giant grizzly. She loved his hairiness and the clay-dust aroma of his worn terra-cotta-stained clothes. The first time his gentle, over-sized hands had touched her, they left big powdery paw-prints on her sweater. With his mark upon her, Lilah had become his in an unspoken way.

Eventually they had found a place of their own in Santa Fe where, since they were both potters, they could share a kiln. But increasingly, to Lilah's discomfort, she felt cut off and alone, more lonely, in fact, than she had ever been when she had lived by herself. As the weeks passed by, the fuzzy edges of her discontent sharpened and narrowed, focusing in to a critical beam on Jed.

She noticed that Jed's nightly after-dinner snooze was beginning earlier and earlier, overwhelming him right at the table before she even had a chance to serve the coffee. Lilah tried cooking lighter meals, drinking less, and talking more, but always his shaggy head would slump forward in gradual jerks until his chin anchored securely on his chest.

Neither the discomfort of the hard kitchen chair nor the clatter she deliberately made as she cleared the dishes aroused him. Inwardly, Lilah raged, wondering why she wasn't the one to fall asleep, leaving the dishes for him to clear. She cursed the silent blackness of the New Mexico nights, the absence of traffic in Santa Fe streets, the lack, really, of anything better to do. And, most of all, she blamed the unrelenting sameness and security of being a couple.

As summer nights lengthened into autumn ones, Jed's naps deepened, and Lilah feared that winter would bring about a full-fledged hibernation. In desperation she began inviting Alan to dinner. Alan was their best friend, a transplanted New Yorker, who crackled with the excitement of an electrical storm. Lilah marveled that his nervous, urban energy had survived intact despite the diluting spaces of New Mexico. Like a broken recorder, he seemed stuck on "fast forward."

At first, the shock of an intruder, even such a familiar one, shortened Jed's nap to a fleeting twenty-second doze that almost escaped notice. But as Alan's visits became more routine, Jed was soon back into his deep sleeps before dessert was over.

"Dessertus interruptus!" exclaimed Alan the first time it happened. "Does he ever do this during entrées?"

"Not yet!" laughed Lilah.

Unable to resist, Alan slipped a half-eaten brownie off Jed's plate and passed it beneath Jed's nose. He whispered: "I am going to eat your brownie. It's the last one." Alan paused a moment, then added in full voice: "I repeat, I am going to eat the last brownie." Jed's eyelids quivered against the weight of sleep, but remained glued shut.

Alan reached across the table, lifted Lilah's hand to his lips, and noisily kissed each finger. Lilah glanced back and forth between the men, delighting in the game. Jed's eyebrows quivered, his upper lip twitched, and his cheeks puffed with each deep, regular exhalation.

Alan rose slowly from his seat and walked to her side of the table. Then, taking her chair in both hands, he tilted it back forty-five degrees and lowered his lips to hers.

His kiss was not the playful peck Lilah expected; it was soft, slow, serious. His gentle lips lingered on hers, as though deliberating, before they opened and pressed on more inquisitively. Floating on the tilted chair with her feet dangling in the air, Lilah would have felt ungrounded except for the ever-deepening kiss. Without thinking, her tongue searched for his, wanting to make the connection stronger, and her toes curled as the kiss permeated her entire body.

Alan ended the kiss as slowly as he started it, orchestrating a diminuendo that made Lilah want to weep. Then he set her chair upright and, quietly and deliberately, returned to his seat. Jed's head flopped too far to one side and jerked him awake with a startled grunt, bringing their game to an end.

In the days the followed, Lilah kept inviting Alan to dinner, anticipating dessert with a particular relish. As soon as Jed succumbed to the nightly spell, she and Alan invented new games. Alan's ingenuity amazed her. Without leaving her chair, Lilah thrilled to new sensations. She nearly shot through the ceiling the first time he fondled her bare feet under the table. He took each foot between his hands and gently massaged the instep. Then he proceeded to caress each toe, one by one. Lilah leaned back and closed her eyes. The tenderness that Alan lavished on each worn callus made her feel totally adored. Suddenly, a velvety warm wetness engulfed her big toe, sending an electrifying jolt straight to her inner core. Lilah opened her eyes and gasped. Alan was sucking her toe.

"Oh don't!" she moaned. "That's too much."

Alan's tongue slithered over and around her toe. With an involuntary jerk, her hand flung out and knocked her wine glass onto Jed's plate, shattering the ecstatic moment.

Still, the vivid memory of Alan's mouth enfolding her toe lingered for days. It reverberated with aftershocks of pleasure and even haunted her dreams. One night she awoke in a sweat: she had been dreaming of chocolate fondue.

In her dream great quantities of the most colorful fruit had been arranged on a platter with the precision of a mosaic. The luminescent colors sparkled—watermelon and cherry reds, nectarine yellow, apricot orange, kiwi green, plum purple, fig black, and banana white. The total effect was incandescent enough to rival the rose window in Notre Dame cathedral. As she lay in bed waiting for daybreak, Lilah made mental notes of all the fruits she would need.

When morning finally came, Lilah secured a date with Alan and promised him the erotic experience of the century. Then, like a shark smelling blood, she readied herself for the food orgy. She began by circling every market in town, stalking only the most perfect fruit. When she returned home hours later, she had a glorious assortment. She washed the fruit, then cut and arranged it on a large tray so that groups of reds, oranges, yellows, greens, and purples converged in a gigantic sunburst. Lilah found the exposed parts of the tray distracting, so she camouflaged them with torn pieces of angel cake. The result was supernatural; her sunburst glittered among clouds!

Excitedly, Lilah began to improvise a fondue sauce. She stirred chocolate bars into hot cream over a double boiler until they melted. Then she dipped her finger into the velvet sauce and tasted. It was good but not yet sublime. She added a touch of rum and tasted again. The sauce was better but still wanting something. After several more sips she decided it needed a dash of instant coffee powder. She sprinkled in a little, tasted, and added a bit more.

Just as the sauce reached perfection and Lilah hovered at the threshold of nirvana, the phone rang. It was Alan saying he was with an important client and—"terribly sorry"—couldn't make it. He'd come some other time.

Lilah stood holding the receiver for several moments after Alan hung up. Disappointment flooded her. Reluctantly, she hung up the phone and took the pot of chocolate from the stove. She licked the spoon. Her sauce was exactly right. She stirred patterns in it and grew mesmerized by the soft folds that kept caving in upon themselves. Fantasies of all the games she had wanted to invent with Alan melted into the dark reality of the chocolate. She sipped a spoonful of the sauce. It slipped down her throat, coating her unhappiness with its soothing warmth. She swallowed another spoonful.

Then, very deliberately, she took the biggest strawberry from the center of the sunburst and dipped it into the fondue. The chocolate was still very warm, and some of it slipped off the cool berry and dribbled down her arm. Lilah watched the rest congeal and adhere to the strawberry before she popped it into her mouth. She dipped some pineapple, and with the chocolate coating, it became something new and wonderful. The raspberries reminded her of the bonbons her grandmother always kept—the ones with the runny centers that she liked to puncture. Chocolate-dipped grapes burst deliciously, and she ate one after another, savoring each juicy explosion. The watermelon balls added crunch, a zesty contrast to the softness of the warm chocolate. The dipped banana slices, in comparison, seemed almost pedestrian, but the more Lilah ate, the more she knew she could grow to love them too. Kiwis in chocolate did not quite live up to their visual brilliance, but the mandarin orange segments proved to be a real surprise, and she ate them all. Steadily, Lilah gorged her way through the nectarines, plums, and figs. Strangely, the more she ate, the less full she felt. The weight of her disappointment had mysteriously lifted, leaving her energized and alert. Her voracious appetite amazed her, and she eagerly devoured all the berries and finally the cake, piece by piece.

By now Lilah's dress was spattered with chocolate. She licked the large spills, careful not to waste a precious drop. Then, very slowly, she lowered both hands into the remaining fondue, raised them up, and watched the chocolate glaze ooze. She sucked each finger, dipped them in again, and delicately pressed a pattern of perfect handprints upon the table top.

As she stepped back to admire her work, Lilah heard Jed shuffling down the back porch steps. Through the window, she watched him find his way around the debris of the summer vegetable garden as he went toward the shed that housed his kiln. Lilah sighed. She hadn't realized how much the garden had suffered. The fragile lettuces had long ago withered to nothing, leaving the vines to take over. String bean stalks now wrestled with yellowed tomato vines. A wilted pepper plant stood apart, barely able to support its abundance of shriveled peppers. Most pathetic of all was an overgrown eggplant. Its leafless branches still bore large, scorched eggplants that sagged like unwanted breasts.

Indian summer was almost over, and the long shadows reminded her that Jed would soon be returning to the house wanting dinner. Before heartburn set in, Lilah knew it was time to move on. She licked a congealed drop of chocolate from her wrist and went to the bedroom to pack her bags.

Lilah's Chocolate Fondue

Nothing satisfies a chocolate craving more sensuously than chocolate fondue, and no time is better for this extravagance than mid-summer when fresh fruit is in its prime. I always find that shopping for the occasion is every bit as ecstatic as the cooking and eating. The sight of row upon row of ripe blushing peaches and apricots and juicy plums is a feast for the eyes. When no one is looking, I reach out and gently fondle the fruit. I like the flesh to feel firm with just a hint of resistance, and I secretly thrill to the touch of peach down or the unblemished smoothness of a ripe plum, plump and perfect as a baby's thigh. Revel in the abundance of the season, and bring home whatever tempts you that day: nectarines, peaches, apricots, plums, strawberries, raspberries, grapes, watermelon, cherries, figs, pineapple, pears, bananas, apples, or kiwis . . . the more different kinds the better.

Wash and peel the fruit and cut the larger ones into bite-sized pieces. Arrange them in a fanciful design on a large platter or tray. For a change of texture you might want to include cut-up sponge cake or angel food cake.

When you can resist the urge for chocolate no longer, set the top of a double boiler over hot (but not boiling) water and combine twenty-four ounces of semi-sweet chocolate with one and a half cups of whipping cream. (You may want to substitute milk chocolate, but I am a semi-sweet lover.) Stir until the chocolate melts and blends with the cream into a velvety smoothness. Dip your fingers in and taste often. Depending on your desire, add four to six tablespoons of rum or Cointreau or brandy and a trace of instant coffee powder (if you want a hint of mocha).

This amount serves twelve chocolate lovers or one binger.

A Gothic Tale

The old house creaked and groaned. A chill wind sent the branches of the leafless maple tree scratching along the windows of the second-story rooms. Every once in a while there was a rushing sound as the wind pushed piles of leaves off the sidewalk, swirling around the carefully tended lawn of the large house. For a moment the sun came out, and a bright light enveloped the elegant Victorian mansion, and then, slowly, thick clouds moved over it and cast the house into a somber gloom.

The front door opened, and a man walked out, wrapping his thick overcoat securely around him as he descended the stairs. He turned and looked at the house for a moment, then walked up the street, soon disappearing from view. A moment later, another man appeared, coming from the opposite direction. He, too, was wearing a heavy overcoat. A small black leather bag was clutched in his hand. He glanced around nervously, then quickly ascended the stairs to the front door and gave a quick tug at the brass knocker. The door opened, and he quickly disappeared inside the house.

They clung to each other in the hallway for a moment. Then, with their arms around each other's waist, they climbed up the long curving staircase of the elegant house.

"You're sure he's gone for the afternoon?" asked the man, his dark, handsome face smiling at her through the gloom of the hallway. She was tall and thin; her long black hair flowed over the red velvet robe as she hurried him into her bedroom.

"Oh yes," she breathed. "Isn't it wonderful?"

He quickly undressed and threw himself on the bed, pulling her down beside him. They lay there for a moment, silently listening to the wind and the creaking of shutters against the large windows. Then, suddenly, they looked at each other and laughed and embraced for a long time. His body lay on top of hers, and her arms stroked slowly up and down his back. She loved his body. It was so tall and slender. The texture of his skin was fine and smooth. His chest was covered with a heavy down of black hair. She liked to caress it with her palm. In some places it was so thick she could wind it around her fingers. Sometimes she gave a little tug with her thin sharp fingers, and he shouted at her in mock protest. Teasing and caressing each other, the minutes sped by.

"Do you like my nightgown?" she whispered.

He looked at her, admiring the pale transparent skin of her face as it set off her large brown eyes.

"Miss Innocent," he teased. For the first time he noticed the nightgown she wore under her heavy robe.

"Oh, I see, playing sick and waiting for the kindly family doctor!" He burst out laughing. "Oh, I do have wonderful medicine. But what is this you are wearing, a curtain?" He frowned wickedly. With a quick movement he pulled off her robe and pulled the thin material of her gown over her head, throwing it carelessly on the floor.

The yellow gauze of the nightgown collapsed in a soft heap beside the bed, lifting and falling with the drafts of cold air that streamed through the big bedroom window. It drifted along the side of the bed, a neglected bit of yellow stuff.

He squeezed her hard. "We don't need clothes. God, your body is so soft and warm . . ." He stopped in mid-sentence. There was a sudden ominous creak on the stairs. They both held their breaths, not daring to make a sound, straining their ears, holding the very blood in their veins still so they could hear better.

Cautiously, he rolled off the bed and crept to the door. He tiptoed to the landing and looked down the stairs. No one there. With a laugh of relief, he threw himself back on the bed.

"Whew, I could get killed!"

He laughed, and she smiled knowingly. It was the danger they loved, the tight merciless danger of being found, making love when it was forbidden. It stirred their senses and made every moment important and intense. They dallied and caressed, their bodies fitting together so perfectly, so gracefully, it seemed they had been made for each other, and not for all the other meaningless people in their lives.

Their lovemaking was passionate and prolonged. They clung together so tightly, a ray of sunlight could not have come between them.

The yellow wisp of gauze danced on the floor, the lonely sunbeam cast out of its place.

Every sound in the old house was magnified, bigger than life, like the family Bible that sat ponderously on the bureau. Relaxing at last against the big pillows covered with immaculate white-starched covers, they stared solemnly at the ceiling. An impish smile flitted across her face, and she suddenly got up from the bed and walked to the bureau. She picked up the heavy Bible, hugging it to her. Laughing delightedly, she fixed her gleaming brown eyes upon him, her long hair streaming over her soft shoulders. The doorway outlined her slender body with the fragile breasts crushed against the heavy book.

The yellow gauze stopped dancing and hunched up in sudden apprehension.

"Yes, judge and jury, I swear it is true," she intoned in mock seriousness. "We dared to do it. We broke the command . . . ."

The yellow gauze crept behind the bed. A gust of wind rattled the windowpanes fiercely and the startled lover half-rose from his icy pillow, a smile frozen on his handsome face, a smile of eternity.

"Yes, ladies and gentlemen, this is the room, the very room, where the heinous murder was committed." The guide pointed to the pictures hanging on the wall.

"This little lady's husband came home and found her with her lover. Enraged, he shot them both with a pistol he always kept downstairs in case of intruders. It was the crime of the century! They found her lying on the floor, right there where you can see the dark bloodstains. She was clutching an old family Bible to her breast. He must have tried to force her to confess or something. And that other picture, that smiling, dark, handsome man, he was the family doctor, a trusted friend. He was her lover. They found him lying on the bed, one shot through the heart. They say he had a smile on his face."

And the wind blows around the corner, and her lover lies there with his slender body, smiling, smiling as the blood washes his life away, and the thin wisp of yellow gauze dances lightly like a sunbeam and the thick black hair veils the luminous body as it sinks to the floor.

"Yes, judge and jury, I swear it is true. We dared."

Grooming Fishwife

Grooming fish, in some species called "damsel fish," enter the mouths of larger fish, even predatory ones, to rid them of parasites and debris. Some of these "fishy" relationships are intimate and permanent; others are looser. Whether both benefit from the relationship has not been conclusively established. The damsel who takes up housekeeping in the mouth of a predatory fish is generally assured of a safe lair and immunity from harm, though mishaps do occur.

Deep in his deepest yawn
I have lived and moved and had my
Being
Like grooming fish lodged in his mouth,
I have picked the debris of countless breakfasts
From his teeth
Sometimes, admittedly, posing as a
Maid
In my starched uniform
To gain entry
Startling him only when, berserk, I
Strip off my clothes
Commit mayhem,
And run, screaming,
Down the red-carpeted hallway of his tongue
With cameras flashing
And women snarling
"She never really *cared* for him, you know."

V. BACK IN MY LIFE

*O*ne distinct pleasure generally denied the very young woman is the experience of having a former lover reenter her life. Each recurrence carries
with it the headiness of previous encounters. Like sexual experience, whether
in the moment or over the years, the ecstasy of the present clearly owes its
richness to ecstasies past.

The first experience of meeting the eyes of one who knew you intimately
in another time, another place, is a piercing exchange in which you both
stand, terribly naked, for an elongated second before speech comes.

You swallow hard and say: "Is it you?"

Then the rituals begin.

"It's been a long time . . ."

"Tell me about yourself now . . ."

"What ever happened to . . ."

If there is any magic left, you arrange to meet again. You prepare yourself for this meeting with elaborate care. The dizziness you felt when years
were compressed into seconds is now exactly reversed: you see yourself in slow
motion, and your self-preoccupation is total. You find yourself protective of
your memories, perhaps unwilling to damage their crystalline containers
with the invasive present. You dress, hiding this a bit, accenting that,
remembering a color you shared like a favorite song. You sprinkle your
appearance with something old, something new, all the while watching new
memories, like embryos, expand and elaborate their delicate features.

When you meet him now, the exchanged look has lost its nakedness. You
are both planted firmly in your present and separate selves that challenge

each other to hold out against the quicksand of nostalgia. You wait for him to push you to the edge of the swirling eddy. He circles cautiously and waits for you. You talk, and—sooner or later—in a sudden remembered incident, you reach out at the same moment, and it begins.

Il Mio Tesoro

I was standing with other students half my age, waiting for the class to break so that we could pile in. We heard the familiar rustling noises inside as books closed and papers were jammed into bookbags and briefcases. Above the rustle, there came loud shouts of the professor trying to give last-minute instructions to a class eager to move on—to the next class, to a café, to a waiting friend. The door burst open, and the students all around me begin pushing their way into the room before those inside could get out. I hung back, waiting for a more civilized moment to enter, when he appeared—like me, distinguished from the others by his age. Except for a more pronounced stoop to his shoulders and a few gray hairs in his sideburns, Giorgio had not changed that much in the twenty years since I had last seen him. He still had the kind of face that in repose was so doleful you almost wanted to laugh. It was a large face, with solemn eyes that stared out at you and a nose that looked as though its maker had intended to come back and finish shaping but forgot.

I said "Giorgio" and he said "Beth" in the same instant and with the same tentative intonation. By now, the other students were coming between us in their scramble to get inside. We moved away from the door and, in quick, overlapping sentences, said all of the dumb things you say when you haven't seen someone in twenty years and can't quite recall the relationship. When I saw that a student was about to close the classroom door, I pulled away from him, nodding in assent to his invitation to have dinner that night. "Yes, here's my address. Fine... see you at seven."

As I showered and dressed that evening, I was still frustrated by how little I could remember of Beth at nineteen and Giorgio at twenty-one. The fragmented memories that drifted in and out of my mind kept getting stuck on the silliness between me and my girlfriend as we vied for his attention at a campus dance.

"I think he's interested in you," she had said.

"Don't be silly, it's you he's been staring at all night."

"I think he's just shy."

"Look at those eyes!"

"What nationality do you think he is?"

I stopped to stare at myself in the mirror, straining to see my face as he would see it, as he *had* seen it earlier that day. Of course I had changed—for the better, I thought. I tried again to conjure up more details of our relationship. When I shut my eyes, I saw him sitting in an old, falling-apart stuffed armchair in my little $32-a-month apartment looking with interest at a drawing I had done. Had we ever kissed? I squeezed my eyes tightly together as though it would help bring him back more clearly. Blank. Nothing.

On the way to the restaurant he had selected, we managed to fill the space with more trivia, interrupting each other in our nervousness and laughing like new lovers. When the waiter left us to look at the menu, Giorgio reached across the table, took my hand in his, and gazed passionately into my eyes.

"How wonderful it is to see you," he said in a husky but low whisper. In his Italian accent, the "wonderful" became "wonnnnnder-rrrful." I found myself confused and embarrassed. It was obvious that he remembered far more about me, about us, than I did. He asked what I was doing now, and I covered my distress by launching into unnecessary detail about the present.

It was clear throughout what turned out to be a long, lingering, romantic dinner that he assumed we shared the same memories. I finally relaxed and treated him as though he were a new man in my life (he might as well have been). If something about the past came up inadvertently, I avoided making direct responses, letting my smile cover my uneasiness.

My distress returned when we got back to my house. It was simpler to invite him in than to stand outside searching like an adolescent for the right parting words. I left him on the couch and escaped to the kitchen for brandy and glasses. I was aware, with mixed feelings, of playing the older woman whose furnishings were a far cry from the hand-me-down armchairs and stacked orange-crate bookcases we all had in those days. I placed the snifters on the table and sat a cool distance from him on the couch. Without looking at his glass or reaching for it, he again grasped my hand in his and said "Darrrling." I took a deep breath and ventured a remark.

"You know," I laughed—lightly I hoped—"I don't seem to remember a lot from those days."

He didn't answer but looked down at my hands, both now clasped in his, and raised them slowly to his lips, tenderly kissing one and then the other. When he finally looked up, he was smiling broadly.

"Of all the memories I have of you," he said, "the one I think about most these many years is going to the little store in the morning to find you a cantaloupe. Do you remember how much you liked the cantaloupe?"

I felt the blood rushing to my face and knew that he would interpret my blushing as a response to shared memories, when, in reality, it was my shock at the implication of what he had said. What is wrong with me? How could I have forgotten so much? I agonized, making a mental note to see a therapist as soon as possible.

As my mind raced in circles, he pulled me to him and, the next thing I knew, his mouth was on mine—full, soft, and sweet beyond description. I melted against him and found myself becoming Ingrid Bergman whose lover's cinematic kiss in some long-ago movie opened door upon door upon door in seemingly endless progression. (Whatever the film, I remember enough to have said to myself: "So that's the way it is!") And now, the 39-year-old woman wanted to feel Giorgio's body hard against her while, at the same moment, the adolescent girl wanted to go on kissing him with the virginal passion that has no further expectation. As for him, he seemed equally content to stay with long, passionate kisses, as though there were no place a kiss need go.

I savored the sense of timelessness I was experiencing and, as the kiss went on, I marveled that his mouth alone could bring me to such a state of excitement. As we stirred between kisses, his lips and cheeks brushing lightly against mine, I caught a glimpse of his face. It wore a delicately pained expression that excited me as much as if he had touched me with his big, warm, gentle hand.

He finally did pull away and, with a twenty-one-year-old's playfulness dancing in his deep, melancholic eyes, said: "Do you still have that lumpy bed?" (adding before I could respond) "You must know how much I would love to find you a cantaloupe in the morning."

The observer in me was taken aback at my boldness as I took his hand in mine and, without hesitation, led him to my bedroom. We flung ourselves on top of the covers and I beckoned him to let me have his mouth again. Only now did he move his kisses from my face to my neck to the vulnerable spot between my breasts, and back to my waiting mouth—all with the same unhurried and tender care, as if, indeed, there were "world enough and time."

Our lovemaking accelerated, yes, but it did so in liquid slow motion, our silence broken occasionally by whispered gasps, barely audible groanings, and muted cries, until, at long last, an enormous peace filled the room. Too languid, too peaceful, to worry any more about how he would react to my obvious repression of our shared past, I asked sleepily whether we had ever "done this" before. Giorgio raised himself on one elbow and looked down at my face, tracing his finger along my cheek and across my lips.

"Tesoro," he whispered, "surely you remember?" He smiled down at me. "You always said I was too fast."

With the word *tesoro*, the locked-up or forbidden memories suddenly avalanched into consciousness. "Tesoro," I cried. "That's what you used to call me . . . 'il mio tesoro.' I remember, Giorgio, I remember."

Giorgio reached for me and we held each other close, laughing like two errant children caught in the warped net of time, unwilling to come home.

Obbligato

It is November. I have come back to England after nearly twenty years of living, an expatriate, in a city of seaweed and mother-of-pearl. Since July I have been back. This gaunt city of London is a felled giant, gray and sprawling, and as crypt-cold as it has always been in my memories. I remember now the city's cold wet tongue licking my legs as I hurried to meet (on Waterloo Bridge with free tickets for a concert in Festival Hall) the man who was then too shy to be my lover.

At that time he despaired of me, finding my seagreen eyelashes and my promiscuity (with its underlying sorrow) bewildering, but now that he is my lover he is full of hope. He has taken me in hand. He is a tall, neat, narrow man, and he wears the same clothes he wore when I first knew him, almost twenty years ago. Then he was a music student, poor and pale. Now he is a famous musician. He is still pale. He lives in a tall, neat, narrow house on the edge of Hampstead Heath, and I spend a lot of time gazing at the poplars that border his garden.

I reflect how unlyrical is our love affair. Within this garden there are many apple trees. Last summer we lay in an uneasy embrace under these trees while apples dropped all around us with dull explosions, like hand grenades. I was tense with the mortal terror of a direct hit, so our reunion (the first in nearly twenty years) across the spiny desert of our respective histories was fraught with suspicion. The falling apples did not worry him at all: it seems he spent all his free time there on fine days, composing harmonies under a barrage of vegetable fire. Of course, I was deeply moved by this fine oblivion to death or maiming. But I grew increasingly alarmed at the precision and timing of the missiles.

We went indoors as the sun sagged behind the poplars, and in the familiar deadening chill of an English house at day's end, we huddled together in a large leather chair. My remembered glamour, he told me afterward, was in contrast to my bright red nose, corpse-white hands, blue cheeks, and to the stockings, sweater, dressing gown, and blanket, which I had borrowed to keep from freezing and throughout which he tore access to my shivering skin. Had he undressed me fully, I would have died of exposure. He took me home, intact, astonished, and more than a little grateful.

Now, in the bleak mid-winter, I spend more and more time indoors, in his house on the edge of the heath, watching the lovely, lilting formalities of his garden change under the veils of frost. His body bursts into flowers and ashes each time we collide in the straits of his narrow bachelor bed; mine retorts like a firearm to his shadow across the light, to his shape on the hanging air. It is so cold. Central heating accepted and installed, English houses are still marrow-cold.

In his house, in the entrance hall, his two great harps loom like cathedrals. Silent, fabulous, phantasmagoric, they are the guardians of his enshrined heart. One harp wears an overcoat and galoshes. They have a pact. He can fall on it without warning, spin it around, heft it to his shoulder like a stunned Sabine and stride away, slamming into his car and driving off at dawn to have his way with it in a recording studio somewhere. The other stands with naked feet in its own spilled cornucopia of strings, scrolls, and languid, drooping curves. It is arch, provocative, and as blatantly, conditionally available as a high-class courtesan.

I am in love with it, of course. I am besotted by its promises. I feel it alive. I flirt with it when he's not present: whispers, glances, smiles, all the minute sensual signals of the body's language. I wish it would notice me. Once I dared a caress: I touched it, lightly, a lover's touch; I almost screamed with the pressure of excitement. I ran my fingers along the thrilling strings and received the clear, low, singing response like a hand on the base of my spine.

But he heard. Oh, no! He came thundering down the stairs. "Strength, darling!" he shouted. "You must *not* be afraid to attack!" And he flung the lovely creature across his shoulder like a fireman making a rescue from a seventh story. I fled to the opposite wall and shrank against it, watching the ritualized ravishment with blood beating in my throat, my skin raw, as the crystalline bubbles of sound filled the room, piling up on the ice-bound silence of the implacable winter dusk.

Oh, he is magical, magical. He is a Pan figure painted on the lid of a crumbling sarcophagus, a mythological projection from the vapors of my own heavy-lidded realms, grappling a sacrificial swan. I know I should pour libations, proffer appeasements, flowers, incense. I feel myself sliding down the wall as a captive creature, possessed at last, completes its ecstasy and is brought to shuddering stillness. I cannot move. My breath binds my feet to the floor and my back to the wall. I wonder if I'm dying. I stare at him, at the priestly reticence of his body taut in the containment of mastery. He is a fossil, he is ancient, an extinct sea-form stretching back in time. The flow of his body is all benign.

When the very seconds are textured (as at times just prior to lovemaking or now, like this), I stare at him, at the sweet, fragile facts that never change: skin like powder polishing his brow, his cheekbones; curls clustering on the tenderness of his nape; the frailty, the endurance of his shoulders and chest in contradiction to the sinewed arms; the muscular, competent, jealously guarded hands. There is too much magic. Too much time has passed. Too many mysteries, enormous, shrouded, are hovering with pterodactyl wings across the oyster light of my deductions. *Who is he?*

He finishes the piece: one tiny gesture—chill as a truth—of his palm upon the vibrating membrane of sound, and the harp falls silent, the room returns, and with it my lover to me. Oh, my magician. I move across to him, sitting at his harp, and as he gently rights it, I slide my hands over his shoulders, under his jacket, and across his chest. I bury my nose in the fabric of his skin below his jaw. I inhale him like fine powder. I enfold him like a snake. He turns his head, surrendering the alabaster mask of his face to my fingers, which press everywhere because I am making memories. Where is my awe of him? In this moment I love him. I dissolve in a storm of fire and roses, lost indeed to clarity and vision, for there are eagles screaming from all my hidden ledges, and tigers are prowling the surface of my skin. The fabric of time has acquired a nap like velvet for us to loll upon; languid, orgulous lovers with age-old pretensions to an ultimate power.

Bernadette's Warthog Pie

This recipe, sifted through the Mediterranean strata of my consciousness, derives from a blameless, pastoral preparation known to the English as "Shepherd's Pie," lauded for its economy of purchase and preparation. In its original form, using mutton, it conjures up rather dismal images of survival: lonely crofts, worn women in shawls stooping over smoking peat fires; acres of heather, and flocks and flocks of eminently shockable sheep.

For me, mutton is a fertile, racy ingredient. The very sound of the word propels my imagination toward all manner of exotic, pearls-in-the-navel culinary extravaganza—couscous, aubergine, choux farcis, petits pois à la menthe.

Yet Americans, alas, respond to the mention of mutton with the same dread as they do the idea of socialized medicine. It is not clear what nameless pox will fall upon our house if I bring mutton past its portals. I have therefore adapted the recipe to the use of ground lamb, easily found in the meat section of the supermarket or ground to your request by that sweet man with the laugh crinkles around his eyes at the corner butcher shop. For two people, a pound of ground lamb is quite sufficient.

Next, purchase one of these exquisite curly cabbages called savoy. They're very round and crisp and of a particularly subtle shade of green. The other cabbages, those pale, tight, smooth spheres, smiling their virginal Mona Lisa smiles, will not do at all. You never feel that you've violated a savoy; it gives itself joyfully and without regret.

Now choose the potatoes. Inhibit, if you can, your desire for those small white globes whose skins roll back at the touch of a thumb; quickly cooked with mint, they are rhapsodic, yielding, and yet resistant on the tongue, but they are unnecessary here. Keep them for another lamb occasion (and Rose the leg woman has one): a succulent three-inch chop, perhaps, jeweled with mint jelly; or a leg of lamb roasted to the palest pink, brushed with tarragon, stuffed with apricots, preceded on the same menu by a sardonic sorrel soup.

The potatoes I prefer for Warthog Pie are the forthright, Idaho kind with rough, clean skins and shapes that exactly fit your hand. Take about four of these, peel them, cut them into slices, and set them to cook covered in a saucepan of water, to which you have added a few grains of sea salt.

Put the ground lamb into a seasoned iron skillet with salt, pepper, and about five cloves of finely crushed garlic. Make sure the meat does not clump into balls; it must be granular and well separated when cooked. Lower the heat under the skillet, and turn your attention to the herbs you will use for seasoning.

I use only fresh herbs, ones I grow myself. If you have an herb garden as I do, now is the time for a pause in the fresh air and the redolence of these aromatic shrubs and leaves. To enter an herb garden is to embrace a trance state, and it is very much a part of the experience of cooking. Take time, then, to select and pick the herbs you will need: rosemary, mint, and lemon balm. Roll them in your hands, and inhale the aromas of the sprigs on your palm. Close your eyes, breathe, relax.

When you are refreshed, return to the kitchen. The lamb is cooked and is bubbling gently in its juices. Skim most of the fat from the liquid, and add one ounce of brandy. Increase the heat slightly. When the agitation in the skillet becomes intense, add four ounces of white wine. Cook gently. Crush the herbs with a pestle and mortar so that the herbs give up their oils and mingle with one another. Add them to the lamb and stir.

Inspect the potatoes. If they yield to the merest stroke, remove them from the stove, drain them, and return them to their saucepan, adding salted butter and a touch of coarsely ground pepper. Pound the potatoes to a velvety smoothness; then add a spurt of cream. Gently tease them with a fork, easing away any rigidities that may have formed, transforming the whole into a supple, yielding mass. Cover the pan, and set it aside. Do the same with the lamb.

Turn your attention to the savoy cabbage. Remove the stem with a sharp knife, and ease each fragrant leaf apart so that it resembles a great green rose. Place it in a colander, and bathe it in a shower of warm water, making sure the base of each leaf is drenched. Shake the excess water from the leaves, and set about shredding them finely, perhaps using one of those curved, two-handled blades that lend themselves so readily to a rhythmic, rocking motion. Use the entire vegetable: the strong thrust of the leafy slivers will subside dramatically when cooked. Cook the cabbage uncovered in about two inches of boiling salted water for about a minute and a half. At all costs, the color of the leaves must be retained; there can be no limp and pallid results. Drain the savoy, and retain the liquid in which it has cooked.

Slowly add the liquid to the cooked lamb, stirring gently and avoiding any premature outpouring of fluid. If the sauce becomes too diluted, thicken slightly with a teaspoon of potato starch mixed to a thin cream with cold water. However, you may want to taste for seasoning before you do this, and adjust accordingly. I would just mention at this point that variety is the very essence of success in this field. Be adventurous and experimental. A slavish obedience to instructions could result in an insipid and disappointing experience.

All is ready for the climax, the union of all these detailed preparations. Select an attractive, shallow dish that responds favorably to heat. Warm it slightly. Spread the cooked ground lamb on the bottom of the dish, then the cabbage in a joyful green layer. Surprise it with a quick squeeze of lemon, and now the coverlet: the creamy billows of mashed potato slightly rumpled, a little disheveled by the fork you use to spread it. Soothe with little dabs of butter over the surface. Then broil briefly until the peaks and troughs are touched with gold.

And now, take off your apron. Step back, inhale deeply. The air around the stove shimmers and becomes translucent. Is this a mirage? What are those silken tents, these veils, these sounds of finger cymbals? Go to your divan, stretch out upon it, and deliver yourself to the expectation of bliss.

The Hot Tub

"Nothing," said the hostess, "nothing ever happens in a hot tub." She had said this reassuringly to Christina as she showed off her new house and not incidentally her new marriage. Christina not only mistrusted Gwen's assurances but wondered why she was the sole remnant of the old crowd to be invited for the house- and husband-warming. Enthusiastically, Gwen had scooped her up from the crowd to pass her around like an hors d'oeuvre: "This is Christina, my oldest friend." Christina realized that the word "old" did not have a particularly valuable connotation with Gwen. Typically, she had not even bothered with her old furniture. Presumably, it had stayed with her old husband or her old job. This time she had not even taken the children with her into another brand-new life. That's how spontaneous Gwen could be. "You've got to keep moving," she used to tell Christina, "or you'll be stuck in a hole so deep that you can't get out." Although she blamed Gwen for all the devastation she left behind, Christina admired her courage to blast off into the unknown.

Christina guessed she had been invited merely to witness this new venture, to learn a lesson from the hostess, who now sat down on a large orange pillow, floating on a white carpet, between white designer tables and flower containers, alabaster sculptures and art deco mirrors. The orange pillow set off Gwen's black designer dress; open to the navel, it exposed her tiny breasts from a seductive angle. Neil, the new husband, made drinks and worked the blender, often kissing his bride on the shoulder.

Christina felt like an antique with her twenty-year marriage, her secure job in the library, her inherited Victorian furniture, and three practically grown daughters, who still lived at home with all their pets.

Would she have accepted Gwen's invitation if David and the girls had not gone off on their annual backpacking trip? She knew that David sided with Gwen's first husband and refused to have anything to do with "that woman." But Christina remained loyal to their lukewarm friendship for old time's sake when she too had been reckless, high-spirited, and nonconformist. Not that she regretted her own choice of settling down, but she couldn't refuse a chance to glimpse Gwen in her newest element.

Finishing her martini, Christina wandered aimlessly toward the swimming pool where several guests splashed noisily. They wore no clothes, which didn't seem to matter because the lights had been turned off. Only candles in glass containers beckoned softly. The martini made it easier to give in to a strange sense of rebellion and curiosity. Christina removed her blouse first, then her bra, a little startled by the breeze that touched her skin ever so slightly. Then she quickly dropped her skirt and panties and plunged into the pool's anonymous darkness.

"I thought it was heated!" she screamed. Her voice was drowned in shrieks and gurgles from the others, who all seemed to feel that safety was in noise and numbers. I don't have a bad figure, Christina thought. Actually I look better without clothes, which is more than Sue or even Gwen can say. They overdo the tennis and the fasting, which gives them that old leather-over-bones look. Christina swam vigorously to give herself a sporty, purposeful air, but the cold was getting to her, as was a large body with a long beard—not her type at all. He seemed to invite sudden collisions by cutting into her lane. When he tried to catch her by the ankle, she decided to take refuge in the hot tub.

It slurped in the darkness, filled with bodies. "One more, make room for one more," they cried gaily, compressing themselves so that she could slide in between assorted legs. A glass of wine found its way into her hand. Somebody began to massage her left calf deftly. The conversation turned from the election to a pub on Piccadilly Circus that everybody loved without remembering its name.

"I remember when it was so full that you couldn't talk, you had to shout into each other's ears, and there was no place to put down your glass," shouted Bob, a political science professor. To demonstrate, he reached behind Christina's back and around her front. More willing hands came across her neck and under her arms, as well as under her thighs. A hand massaging her calf moved up to her thigh and fumbled a bit, trying to move higher. Christina was too busy interlacing her hands with arms and legs to be able to interfere with that hand, even when it no longer rested quietly but felt its way deeper, accompanied by the thrust of a Jacuzzi jet. Closing her eyes, she barely listened to the cocktail-party voices, concentrating on her wish that the hand on her thigh would continue to fondle her crotch. It was so easy to enjoy the play of an isolated hand extended from an unknown body. Then she felt a second hand around her waist, and a third began to make delightful rounds between her breasts and her stomach.

It seemed only courteous to pass along somebody else within comfortable reach. To her surprise, she found a woman. The sensation of touching a breast surprised Christina. It was different from her own—longer, softer. "So that's what a man feels—maybe the one who now touches mine," she thought in a rather detached way. Her own breasts were definitely in the hands of a man. The woman gave no sign of encouragement to Christina. Maybe she preferred to ignore what was happening to her. Maybe she too savored it all in utter concentration.

After her initial exploration, Christina found it impossible to pay further attention to her passive neighbor. There was something disturbingly familiar about the playful hand under her buttocks. Keeping her eyes closed, she felt for the arm that belonged with it. But before she could get much closer, the hand took hold of her own and guided it to a penis, which quickly hardened in her politely accommodating fist. "Hi there, how are you?" said a very familiar voice. Her heart skipped a beat. She pulled back her hand as if she had touched fire. Only one person in the world said, "Hi there, how are you?" that way—Stephen.

"It's you," she answered tonelessly, refusing to open her eyes.

"You didn't know, did you?" he asked triumphantly.

"I guess I did, but I didn't want to," she sighed, remembering their last partings. Through all these years the memory of her pleasure with him was as sharp as the pain that lingered after each encounter, so that once and for all, she had decided to stay away from him. The price was too high.

"We must stop meeting this way," he chuckled.

"I thought we had," she replied dryly.

His hand came back to her. She did not push him away. He gently flipped his fingernail against her pubis. He remembered. There was no man who knew so well what turned her on. Sometimes his expertise annoyed her because, like all experts, he took great pride in his work. Sometimes this was exactly what she wanted. She would fling herself on the bed anticipating what he would do, high, before he even pulled her panties off. There were so many variations to each meeting, to every game they played. Sometimes they only had a few moments in the car; sometimes they stayed together for a day. Sometimes they saw each other surrounded by other people; then every word was meant for the other. They had a wide scale of special innuendoes that nobody else could understand. The knowledge that he was never hers, except for those brief moments, created a special passion. The memory brought tears to her eyes. They mixed with the steam of the hot tub. "Passion," she thought, "I had so much passion."

All this time the other bodies purred around them flirting, splashing, climbing in and out. Gwen shouted from the far end of the garden that dinner was being served. One after another they heaved themselves out of the water. Automatically Christina got up to follow the dripping contingent to the house.

"Stay." Stephen held her foot anchored to the bottom of the tub.

"I can't," she protested, "I must go."

"We've never done it in a hot tub," he insisted.

"We didn't have hot tubs then," she couldn't help laughing, although the tears kept coming.

"Well, then, we owe it to ourselves to give this a try. It's a first for me. We don't have them in the East, at least not where I hang out."

"And where is that? The last I heard from you, you were in London. You sent me a postcard of the queen."

"We didn't hit it off. I have a nice place in New York now, a condo near the Cloisters; why don't you come with me?"

"How long do I have to pack?"

"'Til tomorrow. I'm leaving on the eleven o'clock flight."

They were alone in the spa. To have him back, to have him one more time, one last time. She sank back into the warm water. He scooped her up in his arms.

"I mean it," he whispered into her ear, "I want you. I want you all the time. There is nobody as crazy as you. You are just about the craziest woman I know. Remember that time when we couldn't wait for a motel, when we parked right behind the library like kids?"

"Shh." She covered his mouth with her hand and licked his earlobe. His face had not changed, though his beard was now gray. If he shaved it off, he would look no different from when they had first met, more than twenty years ago.

"The first time you said that you were also going to New York, to Columbia, remember? They offered you a fellowship. You told me to pack my things and be ready the next morning."

"You weren't."

"How could I be? I hardly knew you. Besides, you didn't mean it. But I came close to taking you up on it, simply to call your bluff. The idea turned me on: bride runs off with best man. I just loved it."

"Did you love me?"

"Of course not. I was in love with David. Having two men was not in style then."

"Neither were hot tubs."

Her head floated on top of Stephen's chest. Cradling her buttocks, he moved her around in circles like the hand of a clock. Time went back, the years disappeared, then it stood still. They had caught up with each other.

"Your breasts are the same—so round and firm. I've never forgotten the feel of them. I can lie in the dark and hold them in my empty hands."

"Kiss them, suck them," she begged. Then she turned over and let him kiss her buttocks and the small of her back. The water made their movements languid, unhurried. Christina's frenzied shivers melted in and out of dreamy stillness. All remembrance of pain evaporated in the resurgence of their intimacy. They kissed their old kiss, their lips brushing softly against each other. Then the tips of their tongues teased while their bodies pressed together and their hands touched those secret places they had discovered long ago. Whether he was with her or not, he belonged to her life. What would it have been without him?

Later, they sat arm in arm in their bubbling kettle, looking like missionaries boiling for cannibals. At least, that's what Gwen said when she found them and brought them back to reality with a tray of chicken teriyaki.

Relics

Rummaging through my childhood room
I retrieve your letters
which have been lying in state these twenty-five years
in a bottom drawer, my private archives.

Wizened rubber bands break open in shock,
and stacks of blue airmail envelopes collapse,
scattering their patriotic shrouds
bordered in red, white, and blue.

Torn envelopes, bent and brittle as moth wings,
guard the contents respectfully,
but flag-covered coffins and six-cent stamps
don't stop grave robbers.

The pages are lined, yellow vellum,
starched and pressed into neat, indelible folds,
inscribed with calligraphy pen
that breaks the rules
and vomits inkblots and soul-felt confessions—
your heart always showing between the lines.

Some letters typed on onion skin
feel like Braille:

the force of your periods and exclamations punctured
the thin membrane, leaving
tiny holes.

I would gladly have traded these scriptures
for your touch,
but the continental distance
and your sentence to boarding school
without bond or bail,
forced this evidence.

We went on to love and marry others,
have children, lose touch,
but your airmailed words lift me up
as much as they ever did
and I float knowing that
we cared.

VI. GAMES WE PLAYED

WARMING UP

In the early days as we struggled to embrace the slippery Muse, Sabina dreamed up writing games to get us started. This playful technique unlocked our sensual imaginations. One of our first games required each of us to fill in a story about a random encounter between a man and a woman. Jenna pioneered with a vignette about a woman at a hotel who inadvertently opened the wrong door and confronted a total stranger. Her pen froze at that point. Nell burst into the room and undressed the stranger like a big wonderful doll. Bernadette was even more daring. She called a cab and whisked him off into the night. Months later, "releasing the lock of the heavy door," Jenna was at last able to face her stranger in the security of her own room in "The Prisoner."

The Room

Dripping rain, with her briefcase in one hand, purse over her shoulder, a sack of books in her arms, she opened the door to her hotel room, stumbled inside, and kicked the door shut with her foot. To her surprise a strange man looked up from the overstuffed chair, his eyebrows in his handsome face arched in surprise too. She blushed and turned to go, realizing she must be in the wrong room. Again to her surprise, the man rose and gestured to relieve her of her packages. She relinquished them gladly and stood there blinking.

He took her coat off, shook it, and hung it up to dry. Then, without hesitation or awkwardness, he walked over to where she stood, bent his head, and pressed his mouth to the steamy place between her breasts.

Instantly she shivered and felt all sorts of unnamable sensations. For surely this could not be happening to her; it must be happening to someone else. She would never let such a thing happen—being in a room with a perfect stranger. But there was his undeniable head of hair just under her nose.

The smell of her own perfume released by her body heat was intoxicating and made her realize that she had never really smelled it before. The sweetness in her nostrils made her forget her usual self. Was she actually allowing the unallowable?

She disentangled herself, went into the bathroom, and leaned against the door for a minute, savoring how she felt—glowing, charged, and single-minded. She decided to give herself some breathing space to get used to the new self. She would postpone her pleasure with a luxurious bath. She filled the tub, threw off her clothes, and stepped in. While she lay there, she heard the muffled sound of his voice on the telephone.

She washed and dried and wrapped herself in his terrycloth bathrobe. She smelled his fragrance on the robe as she tied the belt, and her head began to reel slightly. She took a deep breath and opened the bathroom door. He sat holding a glass. When he saw her, he leaned toward the table, filled another, and handed it to her. She took it, brushing his hand lightly, and sat down across from him. They exchanged no words. Her fantasies filled her mind. She wished she knew his fantasies.

She was more aware of her body than ever before. She felt her nipples straining against the terrycloth as her breathing became heavier and more in her chest than in her belly. She could not control the tensing and relaxing in her groin.

Her attention was diverted by a knock at the door, which brought dinner on a rolling table, complete with candlelight and wine. She ate lustily, exchanging a few long glances, but mostly attacking her food voraciously.

Before dessert, he stood up, came around to her, and pulled the robe down over her shoulders. She stood up unselfconsciously, and the robe fell to the floor. He took her into his arms and gently pressed his body against hers for a long, long time. Headiness overwhelmed her— she, totally naked, he, fully dressed.

The candles burned down. The room was perfectly dark. The prospect of playing a new role excited her. Very slowly she released herself from his arms and unbuttoned his shirt. When she had removed all of his clothes, she led him to the bed and pressed him down. Lightly, she stroked every part of his face and then down his body, finding his state of full erection incredibly exciting.

In turn, he stroked her body with his lips and tongue. His tongue and breath in her ear shut out all other sounds. Her pleasure at some moments became acute pain. Her head rolled from side to side; her legs drew up and fell apart. He brought her to the brink of orgasm with his tongue, and then entered her with the first near-violent gesture of the night. They both came instantly, moaning and aching with pleasure.

Stillness for almost an eternity—maybe even sleep. She stood, as light was beginning to enter the room. Once again she bathed, then dressed and quietly left the room with her coat, her briefcase, and her books. Her first workshop was to begin in two hours—time to become herself again.

Night Riders

Although he had given the cab driver the address in English, and then again in French—as though both languages had equal subservience to the fluid dominance of his own—she realized that she had no idea where they were going. The taxi was going very fast; the rain whipped against the black cab windows, splintering the lights of the ancient city into neon arrows. She felt immense liberation and joy, a sense of power, that surpassed the fear that whitened her clenched fingers and fluttered in her stomach. Her face felt stiff, and her eyes were stretched wide. The cab was evidently driving near the city's docks. She could smell the sharp, female odor of the ebb tide and hear the foghorns blaring into the night. Sea images swirled in her mind: barnacles silent and exposed on the pilings and algae floating like wet hair in the phosphorescent, sucking water.

She loosened the collar of her sheepskin coat and turned to look at him, at his familiar, unknown bulk beside her. Again she felt the surge beneath her skin. Entranced and as yielding as wet wood, her being flowed toward him as relentlessly as the flickering water in the river's mouth. She felt herself a mass of contradictions, a witch woman, as ancient as the moon but also as young, as silken, as miraculous as a crocus through the snow.

She made a quick, involuntary turn in his direction. She felt wonderful. She wanted to laugh and clap her hands and bounce up and down on the worn leather seat of the taxi. She wanted to creep inside his heavy coat with its close-curled astrakhan collar and burrow like some hedgerow creature next to his skin. She shivered, and a small cat sound escaped. She felt the thrill of the unknown, of adventure, coupled with the splendor of expectation that all was possible. She felt she held her life in her hands like an old and precious coin at the same time that a high, thin voice in her head sang of danger, of risks to serious to contemplate. She felt herself inside her skin and behind her eyes and beneath the tight tethered net of her hair. She wanted the taxi ride in the wild wet night to go on forever.

It did not, of course. Very shortly they stopped before a large, dark building almost invisible through the driving rain. Vaguely, she discerned steps and pillars, an air of genteel decay. He paid the driver, and they alighted. Then they were hurrying (heads bent, his hand lightly guiding her elbow, her feet in their absurd heels clicking in the stabbing rain) around the side of the house. She was aware of bushes, a small shed perhaps for tools, cobblestones beneath her feet. Then a light in a window, and they came to a halt before a low, wide door.

He fumbled for a key (his first gesture of uncertainty in their acquaintance), swung open the door, and urged her inside. She stepped across the threshold, shaking out her hair and blinking raindrops from her eyes. They were in what was obviously a studio, separated from the main house. A fire burned low and red in a large hearth, its light revealing rafters, a skylight, a spacious couch. Easels, stacked canvasses, the pungent smell of turpentine, draperies—all these filling her with happiness—were discernible through the red shadows in the room. She felt chalk crumble beneath her foot as she drew off her gloves and turned to him with a smile of pure radiance.

With quick, urgent movements, he unbuttoned his coat and let it fall. Then he eased her coat from her shoulders and tossed it aside, and deliberately, with the tenderness of enormous and conscious strength, took her in his arms. She responded at once, a total capitulation: his bulk and the contradiction of his gentleness as he brought his mouth down on hers filled her with such liquid desire that she felt her skin would peel back and reveal her bones. His hands moved about her body with competence and power as the kiss continued. Her spine melted and curved into his, and her hands on his face grew urgent, frantic, so that he put her away from him, into the curve of one arm, to undo the buttons of her dress.

As her skin bared to his touch, it seemed charged and alive, and she quivered and jerked in his arms, making her small cat sounds, as the big blunt fingers spanned her breasts and caressed her throat. He urged her gently toward the couch and pressed her back. Her hands reached out to him as he stood above her pulling off his clothes. He knelt over her, pulling off her remaining undergarments, and she was amazed, spellbound by his grace and deftness, his swiftness in disposing of the final flimsy barriers. With each article he removed, she became sleeker, more fluid, as if her flesh were turning into molten gold. She could see its patina in the flickering light of the fire. Her legs, as she flexed and stretched them, raising her hips and arching her back to facilitate his efforts, had the lithe lines of a dancer's, the insteps arched and gleaming.

She was suddenly aware of her own allure: the sheen of her body, the pale arc of her throat receiving his mouth, the lovely, languid motions of her limbs, her breasts bursting like blossoms, her mouth a bruising flower, her head turning on the cushions with the aching restlessness of bound passion. She touched her skin and felt its fine-grained, flowing softness. She touched her lips and breasts and the flesh inside her thighs and marveled at the texture of her body. And as her hands went from her body to his, it seemed to her that she could not be certain where the one began and the other left off. In a way she had never known, she felt herself magnified through his hands. She thought: I am beautiful, I am desirable. Then she raised her arms over her head and arched her back and opened her body. He covered her then; he entered her and, as she caught her breath on a cry, slowly and rhythmically began the deep thrusting that brought her soul springing through the top of her head like a fish from a wave. She watched herself spin away from her body into the blackness beyond the velvet light of the studio room, bright and thin, a fine silver wire glimmering, unraveling, into the lonely, filigreed fog-horned night.

The Prisoner

She lay across the bed and leaned on one arm. The heat outside was intolerable. In her shorts and halter top with the air-conditioning blowing on her, she felt relaxed and dreamy. She undid her sandal straps, letting her shoes fall carelessly to the floor, and then, slowly, she reached for the twenty-five-cent paperback novel she had just bought at the university store. She had heard of the author but had never read his stuff. She opened the book and read idly, her mind wandering a bit. It was so cool here. She had looked at the workmen in the courtyard as she entered the building—big strong men with sweat glistening on their faces. They worked slowly and methodically, and she had admired how masculine they looked despite their monotonous work. She smiled at the memory.

The characters in the book were two young men talking about going to college to beat the draft. One said: "I can't feel guilty about beating the draft. I can't help those who can't, and I don't want to commit suicide. Anyway, John Kennedy said life was unfair." Yes, she thought lazily, so...

She was startled by a sudden rapping on the door; Kurt wasn't due from class until five. It was only 3:30. She moved off the bed slowly. Maybe he'd left early. She pushed the center of the doorknob, releasing the lock on the heavy door. Almost immediately it flew open and a large male figure pushed past her, pulling the door shut behind him and locking it. She was too startled to speak. She had the impression of a big, good-looking man who was worried. In an urgent voice he said: "Give me something to drink."

She blinked but felt strangely unafraid. Moving away from him, she said, "I don't have any beer, but I can give you some juice." He nodded, looking quickly around. There was no one else there. He seemed reassured. She wasn't screaming. He drank the juice she offered and then held out the glass for more. It was a small gesture like a child's. It took away her fear and made her feel in charge, like a mother with a thirsty child.

She shrugged and smiled, gesturing to the worn couch.

"Well, sit down."

He didn't look like a rapist or a strangler, just unexpected company. She sat down on the chair facing the couch and smiled at him. Hmmm, yes, good-looking and masculine. His head was good, his features irregular but pleasing. She conjectured, laughing Irish eyes, good strong workingman's arms. He wore jeans and a cotton shirt, all light blue like a uniform. She began to understand.

"You escaped from the work from," she said matter-of-factly. He nodded his head in assent. He seemed tired and glad to sit for a moment in a cool, friendly room. She thought, He's nice, intelligent, hard-working, and his father was a drunk. Aloud she said: "Got a plan to get out of here?"

He was surprised at her coolness.

"How come you ain't screaming?"

She shrugged. She answered sarcastically: "I think all the criminals are running around on the outside."

He looked surprised again.

"You're damn right about that!" He looked at her more carefully. Thin and blonde and lazy-looking, with her hair falling all over her face. Tanned arms and legs. Her halter top hung loosely as she sat. It did not escape him.

"Man, you sure got knockers!"

She felt pleased. No one had noticed that for a long time. She looked at him speculatively. Kurt wouldn't be home for another hour at least.

"You haven't seen a woman for a long time?"

He snorted. "Two years I been locked up in that hell hole. Oh, I seen women. Bible-toting bitches. They come to see you with their boobs all held up by wires and wave them at you, and if you look a little and believe a little, they might put in a good word for you so you can get paroled. Bitches!" He snorted again in frustration. He looked at her openly. "But I never seen a soft yellow one like you."

She got up, lit a cigarette, and offered him one. He sucked in gratefully and leaned back against the chair.

"And legs, believe me, you got legs."

"These Bible women," she asked, "did they have legs?"

"Oh sure," he puffed again. "They had legs"—a short pause—"and cement crotches!"

They both burst out laughing at his unexpected poetry. He shook his head and smiled.

"Your crotch ain't cement. I shore bet it ain't cement."

They savored the thought. It was so quiet. The muffled sounds of cars outside, the humming of the air-conditioner. They felt isolated and alone in their own little world of understanding and acceptance. He could only stay one hour, and then he would have to run. His destiny was set. He would always be running. Hers was set too. She would always be alone, waiting. Her beautiful body would always be taken for granted and never really seen or felt or tasted.

She stood up and sauntered about the room while he gazed appreciatively. Cement crotch? She giggled and he laughed too.

"I used to think about girls like you, all blonde and away from me. No one I could ever touch, with big white breasts and little nipples hard..." He stopped talking. She had undone the clasp of her halter and thrown it off. She came near to him and held her breasts in her cupped hands.

"Like this?" she teased softly.

He reached out instinctively and stroked the firm, white skin, and then, suddenly, she was all wrapped up in him. They were a gasping tangle of arms and legs and skin and hair and breaths moving back and forth like their overturned bodies.

They were together a long time. Their destinies seemed suspended. They had been given an hour's reprieve, and their hands and mouths stroked, felt, searched. It was as though they were tasting nectar fed to them from outside time and space and rooms.

She stroked his hairy chest for the last time and got up. They dressed silently. He looked out the window. No one there; he had to run again. She looked at her wristwatch. Almost five. She would have to wait again.

They moved to the door, their arms clasped around each other's waists. He kissed her once.

"You got a name?" he asked softly.

"Yeah, I got a name."

And then the heavy door had opened, and he disappeared as quickly as he had come. She went to the window and watched him run across the courtyard. He stopped once and waved—his mouth moved and she could make out the word.

"Angel," he said.

THROUGH A MAN'S EYES

*R*eady for a further stretch, we dared each other to flex some unused muscles and to write from a man's point of view. Sabina teased Rose for always setting the stage and backing away from the climax. In the guise of a man Rose felt free to go "all the way" and as a gift to Sabina wrote Fever. Sabina, too, put her hero flat on his back and gave him what he'd always wanted.

Fever

Z-a-a-a-a-a-p! I'm hit. A broken man. A stab of sunlight pierces my retinas. Z-a-a-a-a-a-p again! The venetian blinds are raised all at once. I recoil like an assaulted sea anemone. This awakening is too violent. Wincing, I see an ocean of mauve. I pull the covers more tightly about my invertebrate body, seeking safety in camouflage. Cool hands touch me on the back of my neck and my forehead. Cool hands, so smooth and gentle. Not the attack I feared.

"Oh, my! You're hot! Awfully hot! Wait!"

She rushes to the bathroom and returns. A damp, cool washcloth, faintly scented with carnation soap, lands on my face.

"Open."

A cold thermometer is placed in my mouth. A cool hand lifts my head while another shakes out my damp pillow. I open my eyes just in time to see her loose breasts framed by the gaping V-neck of her T-shirt. They flex each time she tugs at the pillow. She straightens the crumpled top sheet and sits on the bed beside me to wait.

She is heavier than she looks. The mattress sags, and I roll toward her. I settle against her large thigh. In its denim casing it is firm and warm as a sausage. The double stitched seams and brass studs can't subdue it. She is brushing back the hair from my forehead in a motherly way. I am seven years old again. Her forearm is plump and succulent. The skin glows with a rosy sheen like a plum. What a juicy morsel! Oh, food—how can I be thinking of food after a night wracked by dry retching, chills, and spasms? I shudder. I'm glad she doesn't talk, glad she keeps stroking my head, glad to be inert beside her generous thigh. The silence and her closeness hide our strangeness.

She takes the thermometer from my mouth. "It's 103. I'll get some aspirin. Think you can keep it down?"

I nod helplessly. She returns with two aspirin and a glass of water. I manage to swallow them, and she smiles approvingly.

"You'll feel better."

I am suddenly disappointed. I will no longer have a reason to be lying here. I will have to be accountable. I will be embarrassed at getting sick. I will apologize for the gross inconvenience. I will brush my teeth, shave, and comb my hair carefully over the thinning spot in back. I will feel guilty for having lascivious thoughts about someone else's wife.

But I am very ill. My fever still rages, and if I move, I may vomit again. I submit to fate, which has kindly placed me between flowered sheets in a sunny room. I lie flat on my back, helpless, a barnacle upon a rock. Blameless, unprotesting, I accept whatever comes to me.

She is standing at a desk now with her back turned. She is arranging flowers in a small vase. The vase has high rounded hips like hers. Pleased, she pauses, sniffs the bouquet, and turns to bring it to me. Her brunette sheen and nutty fragrance envelop me.

Something stirs. Twinges deep in my groin remind me I am not a barnacle. My soft underbelly has no protection. I have no shell to close over my growing erection. The sheets rise to a point. I gaze at a billowing circus tent.

She laughs and whispers "Big Top" and gently grips my penis. It does not go down. Smiling, she rolls back the top sheet, then firmly wrestles my distorted jockey shorts down over my erection. She lifts my hips easily—how strong she is!—and slides my shorts off. Then she leans over, places a warm hand beside each buttock, and begins to kiss my penis. Her shiny brown hair cascades over my belly, and I touch it to be sure it is real. Her tongue is tracing Corinthian scrolls upon my incredible column. Will it stand intact, or will it crash to earth in great chunks to be worn away by wind and rain? I am in awe of myself, of her; my prowess, her boldness.

She stands up and removes her T-shirt. Her breasts spring free before the shirt clears her head. I eye the menu greedily: ripe melons, translucent plum skin, and fragrance of roasted nuts. I will have them all. She unsnaps her reluctant Levi buckle and rolls down her jeans. The seams have left indentations across her hips and thighs. I run my fingertips over the soft, narrow roadways as she climbs onto the bed and straddles me. Her pubic hair is straight and shiny, and I watch it slowly lower over mine. Bit by bit I see my shaft disappearing from view. I close my eyes and explore her warm, wet, welcoming vault. We are architectural masterpieces! She leans over me and presses her breasts to my burning face. I am being buried alive, how alive! I breathe in my fate, succumb to it, and hope this cure will never end.

In Praise of Pantyhose

He rarely spent the night with a woman any more. But he was stranded with this one until he could get to a gas station. He wondered whether she had slept next to him. He was alone now between green satin sheets. If only he could make a quick exit. What time was it? His watch said seven o'clock. The gas station opened at eight. He felt his face; he needed a shave. He heard water running. She was in the shower. He had to get away before she came back. He was sure they had slept together. At least he remembered that much and that they had talked. No, he had talked and talked and talked. Good God, what a fool he had made of himself. Just because he couldn't get it up. What the hell did he care? He didn't have to make it with her. She wasn't all that special, just a nice girl who patiently listened because she didn't have the guts to tell him to get lost. Christ, he had spilled his guts out—about the promotion he wouldn't get, about Helen suing for more child support. And then he couldn't get it up, or was that before? Could he have tried twice? She had even tried to help him, very graciously, the perfect lady. And then, when he had finally left, his car was out of gas. Out of gas, the perfect irony.

She had watched him from the window. There was nothing he could do but accept her invitation to spend the night—insisting that he take the bed. Well, she too had slept in it; she had fallen asleep before he finished talking. No, he could not face her this morning. She wasn't his type, maybe that's why—no! Be honest, he told himself, it's not the first time.

"I have to get up early," she had told him before dropping off to sleep. "Just stay in bed until the gas station opens. Don't forget to pull the latch."

When he noticed that the shower was no longer running, he panicked. The door opened. Quickly, he pretended to be sleeping. She approached the bed to check on him. Noiselessly, she moved away. He heard her open a drawer. The more carefully she went about, the more nervous he felt. Finally he peeked at her with one eye. She was naked: a perfectly shaped back, narrow waist, and a fine behind. He could see her breasts, too, in the dresser mirror. They were long and pendulous; he liked them round and small. She had taken her clothes off last night, but somehow he had not noticed what she looked like. She looked better in the morning. She looked very good from behind.

Yesterday he had not seen her from that angle. He had taken her home because of her face. It was the only face at the party that was alive. Dull faces, dead conversations, tired jokes, and stale drinks marked that party. Could be that he hadn't been in the mood. He should stop going to parties just to avoid being alone.

She studied her face in the mirror, penciling her eyes. So that's how they started, with the eyes. He hadn't even noticed that she wore makeup. What had he noticed? A serious face, not pretty, certainly not striking, but intelligent. The face of an efficient secretary or nurse, a face that blended unobtrusively into the work atmosphere, one that could be trusted. He would have hired such a face for any number of demanding jobs. But he would not have made a pass at her.

Oblivious of him, she painted her face with slow and deliberate care. What kind of work did she say she did? He couldn't remember; maybe he hadn't asked. Different instruments went with different processes, it seemed. Delicately she lifted something with tweezers and guided it to her eyes—lashes. She glued them on one by one. It took her forever while the clock ticked away on the mantel.

He suddenly became impatient with her for taking that much time with herself, for being so absorbed, so removed from him. She was still not finished. Now she sat down sideways from him. Her hands passed through a pair of pantyhose. When she pulled up her leg, he felt an unmistakable jolt in his groin. Desire was stirring in him, making him swell.

She had long and muscular legs; she danced. She had told him about her dancing, but she was not a professional dancer. The pantyhose melted over her foot and ankle. When it got as far as her knee, she lifted her other foot and repeated the same procedure. Then she stood up. Bending over slightly, she painstakingly pulled and stretched the sheer fabric over her thighs and finally her buttocks. She turned around to examine her work in the full-length mirror by the door. He could see her pubic hair through the hose. She wore nothing else underneath. By now he had a real hard-on. Something bothered her; the seam was a little crooked. She pulled the pantyhose down over her buttocks, spreading her legs slightly to keep her balance. This drove him wild. She did not rest until the seam fit perfectly over the crack—a neat demarcation line finally traced her cleavage separating one cheek from the other. But there was more to come. Bending down again—the cheeks stood well chiseled within confines—she tied the straps of her high-heeled sandals to her ankles. Her light brown hair tumbled over her swaying breasts.

Sweat poured from his pores into the cool green sheets. High-heeled and tight-hosed, she stalked back to the dresser to fetch her bra—a flesh-colored lacy bit of nothing that fastened in front. The effect had to be checked and rechecked before it was covered with a matching slip. This had a slit all the way to her crotch. What followed made him suppress a laugh. Her punctilious art work eventually disappeared under a sober brown skirt and sporty white blouse. She was ready to go to work—the perfect machine, all tuned up for a day at the office. Why did she go through all the trouble? What was waiting for her at her destination? Who would see that perfectly straight seam under her skirt?

At the door she hesitated. Surely she could add nothing further to her disguise. She could. A belt had to be pulled around her waist, a dab of perfume still waited for her earlobe, and one more stroke with the brush pulled her curls down over her forehead. Then she smiled at herself—pleased, comfortable, ready to face her perfect day.

He couldn't stand it any longer—he wouldn't let her go to that perfectly groomed desk. There was nothing he could do except catapult himself out of bed in her direction. He didn't care that he startled her. Before she could resist, he ripped off her blouse, zipped down her skirt, and stripped the bra from her shoulders together with her slip until she wore nothing but her pantyhose. Then he carried her over to the bed and dropped her on top of the green satin—a mermaid in a green pool, her tail shimmering under silky scales.

"I've got to go," she laughed.

But he could not let her go to work. He must conquer her, possess her, devour her. He must set her free. He struggled valiantly with her pantyhose. But each time he managed to pull them halfway down her beautiful ass, she slipped away from him.

Two hours later, he said dreamily: "I'll get some gas now and drive you to work."

"Oh, that's all right," she smiled. "Today's my day off."

RSVP TO HENRY MILLER

Because Henry Miller epitomized the male point of view, we decided to read aloud from Tropic of Cancer. *Half the ladies fell soundly asleep. Sabina and Jenny chose to respond in kind.*

Solo Virtuoso

Ruth dropped the book on the ground and settled back in her softly padded chair. After the morning fog, the sun felt hot. Leisurely, she peeled off her jeans and pushed her T-shirt up over her bra without taking it off. She enjoyed soaking in the sun like that, sensing with pleasure the difference between her exposed and unexposed parts.

The telephone rang. She let it ring—a newly acquired skill. Earlier in her life she would never have had the nerve to hold out against ten repeated demands for attention.

Peace today, peace for a whole day. Nothing could reach her unless she desired it. On one side of her garden, brambles and a mixture of native and exotic shrubs walled off the neighbors, and on the other, a majestic stand of redwoods. The landlady had shown her the patio first, probably to justify the exorbitant rent. "Look at those trees—redwoods from the original estate! It used to be a private summer retreat before it was subdivided."

Ruth sipped her wine, Stag's Leap 1979. Drinking good wine by herself was part of her Sunday ritual. Then she loosened her bra and pushed her panties down to her knees. Lying in disarray excited her. It made her feel wanton, wicked. It was so simple to please herself. Today she would take her time—no rushing, no impatient staccato stroking, just a gentle tugging at her pubic curls, a soft tracing of her clit. The sun licked her nipples, her belly, then greedily penetrated her thighs, urging her to open herself wide.

"Are you pleased with me, sun? Do you like what you see?"

Ruth took pride in her healthy, well-functioning body with its ample breasts and strong hips, the same pride as others took in their cars. She took good care of it too: her skin was taut, her muscles tight from regular exercise and running.

Reaching for her flask, she barely lifted her head, leaving her legs loosely spread to keep her excitement simmering. Then she wiggled her toes, rotated her ankles, and tightened her buttocks, breathing fully with her stomach, yoga style. She let her hands rest on top of her face, loving the smell of herself from "down there." Slowly she removed the remaining pieces of clothing and turned her backside toward the sun. The blaze caressed her shoulders and the whole length of her spine. It kissed her buttocks, entreating her to surrender more of herself. Crouching on her knees she allowed it to penetrate her from behind as her mound arched toward her hands, wanting to be stroked and teased. Subtle variations turned into a strong rhythmic rocking of her body to the beat of her sliding fingers. In . . . in . . . in . . .

Climax crept up on her in tingling waves, each announcing the next one before subsiding. Finally, her whole being contracted into a ball of fire. She was giving birth to her own pleasure. Exhausted she sank back into blissful relaxation.

Resting between sleep and heightened awareness, she suddenly sensed that she was no longer alone. Perhaps it was the slight breeze that sent a frisson up her spine. Sitting up, she discovered a figure in one of the redwood trees. It was a man.

Agile and muscular, he climbed down the tree trunk as though he had done it many times before. She covered her breasts. Too late—he jumped ten feet onto the patio. Only now did she notice that he was wearing a uniform. What war? What country? Fear paralyzed her voice, but her mind was racing through a number of possible defenses: I'll kick him in the groin, she decided.

He remained firmly planted right where he had landed.

"Whore," he spat out, "I know what you want. You want my cock right between your legs. You want me to grab you down there, take you like a man, a real man. You want a man to grab your bushy twat. You crave it, don't you? My prick in your cunt?"

When he moved closer, out of breath and perspiring, Ruth sensed something helpless about him, some trace of defeat, of battles lost. She noticed that two buttons hung loose from his jacket and that his shirt was rumpled. His obscenities, like his uniform, no longer convincingly displayed power. She began to see him as more pathetic than danger-ous, but she stayed on guard. What kind of charade was he putting on? Impulsively, she offered him her glass. He drank thirstily.

"Slut, don't think I don't know what's going on . . . lying there with your pussy in the air, begging for it. I guess you know your busi-ness. Believe me, I do a good job too." Hastily he unzipped his trousers. "Here, feel my dick. I bet you don't get that every day. I bet you haven't had a good fuck for a long time, not with a real man. What do you say to that, eh?"

Ruth recovered her voice. It sounded cool.

"A real man, is that what you are?"

He lunged forward. Hovering over her, he grunted: "Take it, cunt."

"I don't want it."

"Cock-teasing won't work with me, lady."

To her surprise he smelled pleasantly of pipe tobacco. The aroma was somehow familiar.

"Please, leave me alone. I'm not in the mood for company."

"You're a whore all the way through. You only do it for money, fucking bitch. Who do you think you are?" Grabbing her shoulders, he threatened to throw himself upon her. It helped her to know that the chair would surely collapse from the additional weight.

"All right, all right," she told him firmly, "but you must do exactly what I say." Startled by the authority in her voice, he let go of her. "I am not afraid of you," she continued, "and I am not a whore." Obvi-ously there was no point in telling him that she was president of the League of Women Voters. "I'm going to tell you what I want."

For the first time, he looked straight into her eyes, puzzled, intrigued, uncertain what to do next.

"It better be good." He lowered his glance appreciatively to her breasts.

"No, don't touch me there. Pull up your pants. Kneel down beside me."

He moved obediently, as if programmed to take orders. She smelled the tobacco again in his thick grayish-brown hair. She sat up straight, opened her thighs, and pulled his face close.

"Kiss me very, very gently."

He obeyed.

"Now lick my cunt—savor it, explore it with the tip of your tongue. Good, that's it. Continue exactly like that. Deeper now, taste me, feel me. Yes, that's it." As his tongue went to work on her, her body twitched and throbbed in immediate response. Pressing his head tightly against her wet crotch and feeling her moisture on his face, she came quickly with a violent shudder. Spent, she kissed the top of his head and released him.

"That was very nice. You really do know your job," she complimented him.

"Okay, my turn now," he grinned expectantly, touching his fly.

"You may leave now," she said, her tone imperious as before.

"Hey, wait a minute—you're going to go down on *me* first, cunt."

"I'm sorry, I don't have the time. I have to get dressed. But you have possibilities. We must meet again sometime." He looked dumbfounded, but he obeyed, as she had expected he would.

Watching him retreat like a good soldier, Ruth savored the frenzy and the power, but she also felt a little ashamed of cheating him at his own game. Perhaps I should call him back she thought but quickly decided not to. She had had enough.

The sound of a car in the driveway startled her back to reality. Doors shut with a bang. Voices called her name. Before she had a chance to cover her nakedness, her grandsons were already entering the garden.

"Grandma, grandma," they yelled, "why didn't you answer the phone?"

"I called all afternoon to remind you that I'm bringing the boys," said her daughter reproachfully as she came out to the patio. "By the way, you shouldn't let them see you in the nude any more. They're too old for that now. What on earth have you been doing all day?"

"Nothing, dear. I guess I fell asleep reading Henry Miller."

"That old fart? Don't tell me you get off on that macho porn. That kind of garbage should be banned," scoffed her daughter as she set down the stuffed animals and blankets the boys required for their sleep-over.

"But it *was* banned," smiled Ruth mischievously, picking up the book. "I smuggled it in from Paris as a student. I was scared to death customs would find it in my underwear."

But her daughter did not hear. She was already halfway out the door.

Animal Lust

"You really are a madonna, Frances. I'm so glad you're not like all those other girls. They're disgusting. I mean, the things they do! They're like animals!"

Hank wrinkled his nose in dismay and dropped down beside me on the high school lawn. I was lying face down on the cool grass, and I was glad my long blonde hair hung over my face so he couldn't see the sudden pink flush that crept up my neck. He had been telling me all kinds of lurid and exciting stories about a party he had attended, a terrible party where the girls and boys had disappeared into rooms and behind couches. I was secretly impressed and dying to hear more.

"Oh, yes, terrible, terrible," I lied. "What else did they do?"

"Well, he put his hand inside her blouse. It was soft and warm, and he even . . ." Hank's voice sank lower, and his whisper was a little hoarse. "He rubbed her nipple, and it got big and hard."

I wanted to pull down my sweater and let my hand fall along the line of my own breast. I wondered what it would feel like to have some boy open my blouse and caress my breast with the breeze flowing over my naked flesh. What would happen to my nipple?

"Now this will really get you, Frances," Hank went on. "After he did that, he ran his hand under her skirt and felt her crotch. And she let him! Can you imagine?"

I could imagine, and the palms of my hands began to feel very damp. I lowered my head even more and let Hank's words slide over me.

"The thing I really like about you, Frances, is that you don't have animal lust."

Years later, after we were married and Hank had become a busy and successful business executive, the storytelling continued. After dinner every evening, Hank would tell me stories as we lingered over coffee.

"Boy, Frances, this one's too much. See, his mistress works the telephones, and his wife is the secretary right now because the other one had to leave. So his mistress brings in this sexy black nightgown, and his wife holds it up and admires it, and he's standing there looking cross-eyed. And now his wife and mistress are becoming friends, and he doesn't know what to do about it. Now isn't that something?"

Hank would whistle, and I would hang onto every word, trying to fill in the details in my mind. Where would they go? To a motel? I would try to imagine the mistress in the sexy black nightgown with her long hair trailing down her voluptuous back. Would she lie on the bed waiting for him to tear the cloth from her big Italian breasts? Or would she be the passionate one and tear the clothes off him? Then I would think of them moaning and moving all over the bed, and I would lower my head so my hair fell over my face and Hank wouldn't see the flush on my cheeks. Hank always ended his stories the same way.

"I'm so glad you're not like that, Frances. You're so cool and restrained and pure. Yes, you really are my madonna."

And then one day, the stories ended abruptly. I stood by the hospital bed and wondered about the kidneys that failed. Pale and weak, Hank reached out for my hand and gave me a final squeeze.

"Frances, be very careful. Men won't understand you. They won't know you're a madonna and don't have animal lust." His nose wrinkled one final time, and then he was gone, and I was sitting at the dinner table again, but this time alone with no one to tell me exciting stories to end my day.

I avoided men completely, although many tried to woo me.

"A gorgeous thing like you can't just wither away," one scolded me. "You're young. Don't let life pass you by."

Finally, I bundled my grief away. It was just a little bundle really. Hank had been my friend, but he had never touched me deeply. I had never felt we were really lovers—not really. I knew there must be more. I knew there was a man somewhere, a man who had animal lust, who was sexy and daring and outrageous and fun and wonderful. Over the years I had painted him, and I knew exactly what he looked like but not where to find him.

One day as I wandered aimlessly through a department store, I saw a lovely sheer blouse on the stand. It was draped over a slender mannequin that was nude. I admired the way the soft cloth clung to her breasts. On impulse, I took the blouse and went into the dressing room and tried it on. I didn't have the nerve to wear it over my bare skin, but even on top of my slip and bra it clung lusciously and gleamed golden in the harsh light of the dressing room. I admired myself dreamily in the mirror, then bought the blouse and wore it out of the store. I felt elated by my sudden purchase and went into a cafeteria for a cup of tea and to think about the wonderful feeling the blouse gave me.

The cafeteria was crowded, so I had to sit at a table with a man, a stranger who was writing furiously on a thick pad of yellow paper. It's funny how things work out, isn't it? As I sipped my tea, I stole glances at him, letting my hair fall around my face in my old way, so he couldn't observe me observing him. What was he writing? I liked his looks—big and rough with lots of character and something else too. I was painting in passion and lust and black negligees and moaning on the bed when suddenly he lifted his head and looked straight at me.

"All of a sudden," he said matter-of-factly, "this has become a beautiful day."

I felt as sheer and sensuous as my golden, silken blouse as he ran his eyes over me and my body, as least what he could see of it above the table top. I could see my kneecap gleaming in its nylon cover. Was that exposed before, or did my hand casually pull my skirt up a little higher? He leaned over and ran his hand along the fine silk fabric as it lay on my arm.

"You have given me a totally new outlook on this day. I'm a worn-out writer; I need inspiration. How about coming to my apartment and having dinner with me tonight?"

He didn't wait for an answer but handed me his card. In a second he had disappeared into the crowd, carrying his yellow pad. For a second I was dismayed, and then suddenly, there he was again, standing on the other side of the window, smiling broadly and silently mouthing "Yes, yes, yes!" and then he was gone again, crossing the street and turning a corner.

I studied his card. He lived near me. I savored my memory of him, and then, with sudden resolution, I decided. I would go.

That night at six o'clock I telephoned him and said just one word: "Yes." Two hours later I sat across from him at the dinner table. My hair was combed back. It couldn't fall across my face, at least not yet.

My golden, silken blouse lay lovingly on my soft pearly skin with nothing else beneath it. I felt as rich and lustrous as the material that clothed me, as elegant as the blue and white chinaware that lay before me, as warm and inviting as the little flames that rose and fell in the fireplace beyond the table. He was no stranger; I had made his acquaintance over the years, painting in each detail a little at a time, so that now he felt completely familiar to me. We sipped our wine and smiled at each other in the candlelight. It was no surprise to learn that he wrote romantic novels.

Later, as the sheer blouse hung carelessly from a chair and the light from the fireplace warmed our naked bodies, I smiled in secret delight as he stroked my skin and murmured, "The thing I really love about you, Frances, is that you have animal lust."

VII. THE KENSINGTON LADIES REVEALED

*W*e are a potpourri of slightly hysterical contradictions: bold, reticent, eager to divulge, hesitant to expose, garrulous, tongue-tied, lighthearted, and deadly serious. All these divergent forces operate at once in each one of us and tend to make our meetings rather raucous affairs. When we do engage in a psychic tug-of-war, everyone wins. Cautious thinkers begin to take chances and find themselves doing unexpected things in the joy of the moment. Impulsive doers who ricochet through life stop to reflect—and regain control. Unwittingly borrowing from each other, we discover new dimensions in ourselves which seep into our stories, weaving our desires and differences into a rich tapestry of collective experience.

Not all of us choose to write. Ann Gordon, Nicola Hamilton, and Judy McBride channel their creativity into ardent listening. Their exuberant comments and continued presence have insured the survival of the group, for without applause and encouragement many of our stories would never have been written.

I have always felt that I am a member of the Kensington Ladies' Erotica Society under false pretenses, waving a flag that isn't mine. I am not a writer. I don't want to write. I loathe writing. I am a sculptor, possibly a painter, and my creative energies naturally flow into visual images.

Three years ago, Sabina, who saw me floundering through the agonies of a very bitter and painful divorce, invited me to join the group. Writer or not, she said, it would be good for me and maybe stimulate me in new directions. I told her that to be reminded of erotica was the last thing I needed at that juncture. It was the one thing I had always felt I would be forever deprived of. But I was curious and lonely, and so I went to a meeting. Soon the group was a major focus of my life.

Everyone was kind and patient, but after three years of constant work by all of the "regulars," I sensed some impatience and frustration with my inactivity. After all, they had freely nourished me, bodily and psychically, with their delicious cooking and bared literary souls. It takes skill to cook well. It takes both skill and bravery, particularly bravery for us who were born into the tag end of the American-Victorian-Puritan era, to expose our erotic imaginings and tentative literary skills to outsiders, even friendly ones.

Needless to say, I had exposed nothing. I was the coward, safely ensconced in my cocoon: "I can't write: I am a visual artist." Parenthetically, I also have the irresistible habit of falling into a pleasant snooze or two after dinner, particularly if wine is served. I am a morning person with a very low alcohol tolerance. Naturally, this is embarrassing, and I have become quite adept at covering my weakness: I catch myself awake just before my head bobs, always sit in high-backed chairs after dinner, and generally fake a nonexistent and spurious alertness.

One evening, after a very satisfying predinner chatter and delicious, filling, and soporific food and wine, I followed my abominable pattern and dozed through the reading of a sketch by a new member. I retained enough consciousness to be aware that I was missing something unusually well written and that I'd be sorry later. But first things first, and after food comes sleep!

I awoke abruptly when the voice changed, and I heard my name. As I guiltily jerked to attention, Sabina was saying, "Well, Ann, what about you? Why don't you do a sculpture?"

In my half-awake state I panicked as visions of very specific and gross images passed through my mind—more in line with the crudest Japanese erotic woodprints with their enormous exaggerations. My sluggish mind jumped to an innocent lady answer, half the world away from Oriental prints. I hinted that Rodin had pretty well exhausted the subject, and in addition to not wishing to plagiarize his work, it would be the greatest arrogance on my part to compete with his genius. They agreed, but Sabina said: "Why not sculpt just part of a body?"—at which point I truly panicked—"like the hands in the story Elvira just read?"

Faster than greased erotica, the various things that hands could do reeled through my brain, and I could find no reason to object. Though I hadn't the faintest hint as to the story's plot, what the hands actually looked like, or what they had been doing, I covered my assorted confusions and guilt by immediately agreeing, on one condition—which I was certain would save me from any effort. I insisted that the original owner be the model.

As a matter of fact, I cannot sculpt anything without a living model, from whom I get an emotional impact. I prefer a responsive mammal to any of the lower orders, and I much prefer a verbal animal, though I have done elephants, horses, butterflies, dragons, birds, and other pets. I noticed that most of the husbands, lovers, and sons of our various members avoid our meetings like Herpes II. If they must come into the house to eat or retire while we are convening, they try to slip in through the back door and are laboriously inconspicuous as they slither or leap to their destinations.

212

I was completely flabbergasted the next day when Elvira phoned to say that she had contacted the subject of "Hands," and he was sufficiently amused and intrigued to agree to pose. Assuming I'd have to endure some conceited, self-satisfied ass whose hands had better be great to make up for the boredom I anticipated, I spent the time prior to his arrival conjecturing every variety of beautiful, graceful male hand in a million exotic, erotic, sinuous poses.

When the owner of the fabulous hands walked in the door, I was speechless. He had a set of the homeliest digits I had ever seen—and homely in a way to which I was particularly sensitive. They were an extreme exaggeration of the rather unattractive bone structure of my own hands, plus an unusual fleshiness and a curious suggestion of something arthritic in the horizontal angle of the fingers at the knuckle joint. His first words were that he couldn't resist the temptation to find out how anyone could make his hands beautiful and sensual. Silently I had to agree, and silently I ditched all my preconceived compositions. I told him it would take me a while to decide on a pose, and, in the meantime, let's relax and get acquainted. I've learned how to set a subject at ease and dive into his or her psyche. To do it, I set up a very intense intimacy that is almost—in fact, really is—a mini love affair. When I am through, it abruptly ends.

As "Hands" talked about his work, I noticed that his hands assumed several characteristic and intriguing gestures or postures. In one, he would hold or, rather, cradle his right hand with his left and seem almost to massage or caress the palm of the right hand with the thumb of his left. At the time I didn't analyze why this caught my eye but simply started to sculpt. I felt I'd discovered what the gesture was saying as I worked.

In the meantime we talked and talked and talked. Since we met for more than one session, I would sometimes "import" a friend to amuse him, as I was now determined to prevent *his* boredom from turning him away before I was through. I knew that he was very busy, and I felt he was in some way impatient or restless.

In the end he was pleased with the enormous size of the finished work. My instinct is always to work larger than life, and for me these hands really are larger than life.

I was born in England of Italian parents and spent most of my life engaged in an internal emotional battle between my Mediterranean temperament and my all-too-well-acquired British reserve. Many years ago I traded in the gray London fog for California sunshine, eventually married an American, and now spend most of my time raising two young, energetic children.

I was educated in England at an all-girls Catholic convent school and suffered the inevitable stifling consequences. So when my friend Rose suggested over lunch one day that I join her Erotica writing group, my ears perked up like a dog who's offered a juicy bone.

Right away I sensed a feeling of deep trust among the members even when different factions appeared to emerge within the group. Best of all, I loved to hear the women talk about sexuality and read their work over good potluck dinners. The energy of the group was infectious and I felt encouraged enough to continue with my own nonerotic writing, which I had firmly put on the back burner with the arrival of my first child. My function within the group has evolved into one of encouraging listener, gentle critic, and unflagging supporter.

Seven years ago I attended the first meeting of the Kensington Ladies' Erotica Society out of curiosity and loyalty to my friend, Sabina. Although it was very threatening to me then, the unexpected is often the sweetest, and I was relieved that I had found a safe place for exploring fantasies. The other women were real people, not silly stereotypes, and I was struck by their beautiful, simple, and humorous approach to such a universal area, sexual fantasy.

As I reread the stories produced from the erotica group, I wish to take up a banner and cheer for the success of my sisters, hidden in this book by pseudonyms, but who hid nothing the many times they revealed their own deepest thoughts in conversation and in writing. I myself made many attempts to put into playful art form my memories and longings. I recounted my own stories to private pages only to bury them in a crumpled ball in the wastebasket. I am certainly thankful that my friends' stories were not similarly wasted.

Growing up in dry southern California in the economic drought of the Depression, I knew every lily pond, birdbath, and fountain in town. There weren't many, and in the bland, dusty, middle-class environment these tiny oases of coolness and mystery were the secret joy of my life.

My public joy was the barefoot life, running with the boys when I could, leading the girls when I couldn't run with the boys: baseball in the street, basketball in the vacant lot, wrestling matches, tree climbing, and swimming in the surf. I was long on daring, skinny and fast, with big strong hands and feet, a tomboy with glasses and straight brown hair bleached blond every summer. I was plain and awkward, but looking back at my pictures from those days, I see an uncertain grace and sweetness trying to come through.

I repressed that because I didn't want to become "such a sweet lady" as my mother. I knew what marched behind the sweetness, and I knew there were no lily ponds there. Her interest centered on my brother, five years older, and she didn't really notice my lack of imitation of until it was too late. I knew she loved me in the abstract, and it baffled and infuriated me. No one wants to be loved in the abstract: if it can't be for the real you of the flesh and the dreams, you don't want to hear about it, or at least you don't want to hear it called love.

At twelve I found my intellect, and it surprised me so much I gave up the barefoot life forever. I'd always read my brother's books—it helped close the gap between us to know whatever he was learning at the moment. But when I started on his high school physics books, the rivalry vanished, and I fell in love with the celestial order of the universe expressed mathematically.

Things moved fast then. At thirteen I was in love with the school genius. I stalked him intellectually, wreaking adoring acts of will on his unconscious. He succumbed, and we sailed out on that eternal lily pond of the very young in love. There were depths there—the power of sex revealed itself to me in my lover's renunciation of it. We caressed endlessly and deliciously, our senses raw with arousal, but never admitting the possibility of fulfillment. In that direction lay the corruption of lust, and we would not be corrupted. But I saw how one glance of the right kind, one voice inflection could spellbind him for more, all the brilliant mind and brave ambition silenced by the eloquence of the flesh.

I knew very clearly then that I would be a daring woman scientist, swimming strongly through the surf of ignorance into the bleaching sun of truth. There would be a secret garden though, full of sensual beauty, the drop of water on fern, the glint of dragonflies over lily pads, the rustle of bird wings in water basins at evening. A man who adored my very shadow even while he achieved his own work of genius would wait there for me, and there our lives would come together in magical union.

At fifteen I left this love for a conventional high school romance, one from which each of us bore the scars of unfulfillment for many years. It was the beginning of the drought of dreams.

At eighteen, in college, reality began to quench the flash of academic promise. It had been launched with scholarships and prizes. Now it bogged down in competition with young war veterans for the sparse attention of overworked professors. My college boyfriend hated my science. Art and literature called me seductively—they were so much easier and more feminine, and I'd always been good at them.

Now I knew where I really belonged, having fun with boys, painting, writing, skimming like the sorority girl I'd become. But just before my twentieth birthday, word came that that boy I'd never gotten over in high school had married someone else. The inner crash I experienced left me a lost soul. Without letting anyone know I was doing it, even myself, I dropped the few remaining threads of ambition and structure in my life and married someone quick to love who seemed to fill the terrifying void.

Decisions like that have their price in lily pond reveries. The unexpected blessing of a child was the last brief oasis before the desert of divorce, financial problems, and child-raising single-handedly.

In time the true, enduring love arrived, but shimmered miragelike just out of reach until patience was exhausted and longing relinquished, then suddenly was mine. Marriage was tried, agonized through, given up, retried. While love somehow survived, the wells of strength were found to be depleted and the imagination dimmed.

Meanwhile there was always the daily living to be made, always at clerical work it seemed. There was the daily life to be kept in order, guarding the residual sanity and the few tenuous family connections. But the dream of intellectuality, creativity, sensuality, so vivid at fourteen, is still dreamed in the late forties with all conviction gone.

On the edge of my unconscious the golden fish dart under the lily pads, a secret fountain murmurs in a grotto, and ancient stone figures are reflected in a mirror pool. The child of drought knows instinctively of a greener land, but not how to get there.

The Kensington Ladies' Erotica Society had been meeting for more than a year when I first met Sabina. Over lunch, Sabina began to tell me about her latest venture—women's erotica. As she talked, I found myself drifting back to my young Hollywood-dominated years when my ultimate heroine was Rita Hayworth—Rita in slinky satin, her long tousled curls caressing bare shoulders, as Gilda, her husky voice curling around a microphone telling me that whatever Lola wanted, Lola got. I started musing about where these sex symbols, as tough as they were victimized, would be in the liberated eighties. I thought of the composite I had made of myself between then and now: a little Rita (I loved perfume, satin, and polished nails), a little Ida Lupino (I pretended to be tough), a little Doris Day (I married and dutifully had children), a little Katherine Hepburn (I insisted on being my own person), and a little "bookish" (for which Hollywood had no model). Now divorced for several years and somewhat unnerved about the possibility of love-ever-after, I see myself as a realist—that is, a romantic to the cynic and a cynic to the romantic.

The attraction to accept Sabina's invitation to the next Erotica dinner meeting was irresistible. The first potluck dinner I attended disappointed me. I had not expected the hours of hors d'oeuvres and chatter about one woman's salad, another's entrée, and another's dessert. Then, too, I saw the other women as more in Marilyn Monroe's generation than in Rita's and mine, and the racy stories I expected to hear turned out to be handkerchief-dropping romance and Victorian-era fantasy. So I thought. Furthermore, aside from the group's rejection of pornographic images of women and Sabina's insistence that our heroines not be shown as victims, I did not find the feminist consciousness I had assumed would be there. (I confess that in some ways that was a relief, for I had found it difficult—though not impossible—to justify my Hollywood image-makers to young feminists.)

In that critical state of mind, I dashed off my first story about a rotten lover. My intent was to be explicit, to come from real experience instead of fantasy, and to present characters with some years behind them. When it came time to read my story to the group, I was suddenly assailed with a mixture of shyness and apprehension. I gave it to Sabina to present to the group, and stayed at home, chewing my long, lacquered nails. From her report, few (if any) of the women found it erotic; "too clinical," "too close to victimization," they had said, although it evidently stirred up a lot of down-and-dirty talk.

I almost left at that point, but writing that story (which for obvious reasons is not included here) had whetted my appetite and, despite the prickly reaction it had received, according to Sabina they had talked about it with animation. I then embarked on "Hands." I wanted to capture, in a torrent of words, the power of a man's lovemaking hands. Again (in my cowardly-lion fashion) I slipped the story into Sabina's hands and stayed at home. And again, there was a reaction—this time more positive, enough so that "Hands" became the stimulus for other "body language" stories.

Perhaps it was the excitement that came from seeing myself as a catalyst that shifted my view. At any rate, I was now hooked. My hypercritical regard for the other women gradually crumbled, and although I remained hell-bent on our coming out with a written product (at a time when eating still seemed to be the major preoccupation), I relaxed my position about what the group was *supposed* to do.

Not surprisingly, I guess, it is only now that I can see the degree to which the "free spirit" I thought I was has been a slave to old forms and images—every bit as much as my more conventional writing mates. And only now do I feel ready to take on the challenge of writing erotica that can stand as "woman-owned"—distinct from Hollywood and pulp magazine prescriptions of how it "should be" for our gender.

I met Sabina one New Year's Day and found her one of the liveliest and most energetic women I had ever met. She said she'd been thinking about starting a group to look at what turns women on and calling it the "Kensington Ladies' Erotica Society." I said I'd love to join. Three months later Sabina called and told me that our first meeting would be at her house. I have strong memories of that meeting. A wonderful feeling for me was that I didn't know anyone really well, and so my sense of safety was from feeling both a trust and also a distance—a separateness. I didn't know where it would go from there; I just thought it would be fun and interesting. Then we started to focus on writing. I would never have written anything if I hadn't been given assignments to write. I felt really nervous at first. If I could write it and then burn it, that would be fine, but the thought of aunts and uncles and grandfathers reading my erotic stories—that was just awful.

When I wrote my first erotic story, I was surprised to discover how *empowered* I felt. In that story the woman undresses the man. I liked writing about fantasies with strangers, but I also like writing about real experiences with my husband of twenty years, as in "Tantric Sex." Our body language stories were inspired by Elvira's "Hands," and mine was pure fun to do.

For a time I was impatient with the group, feeling that we were all too inhibited—not enough *fucking*, for god's sake. I found that down-and-dirty was most erotic to me, but it isn't easy to write or to sustain good erotica. I learned that there can also be eroticism in atmosphere and even in humorous situations.

Most of all, I've loved the sharing of stories, food, wine, and laughter. I've learned a lot about myself in this joyful process.

Ever since I was a child—an only child—I have been spinning out fantasies and telling stories to my friends. At the age of forty I suddenly found myself in a mood that recalled in a way the time when I was ten years old. Tied down by commitments to family and work, by daily routines, and by my strong sense of responsibility, I once again wanted to escape to my own fairyland where everything was possible, where anything could happen. So I sat down and said: "If all your wishes could come true, what would you wish?" That I picked erotica as my fairyland seemed appropriate because in mid-life I was curious again about the mysteries of sex, about my own body and other bodies, and, as in the whispering times of my youth, I still rebelled against authority. I no longer wanted to follow the prescriptions for so-called sexual fulfillment. I even doubted whether there was such a phenomenon as an erotic turn-on.

When the Kensington Ladies rallied around me, I felt again like part of a gang. Comparing my vision with theirs made them sharper, more daring, more exciting. By writing stories, my fantasies took on real dimensions, and I began to look on real life more as fantasy. The sight of a long-lost lover still gave me the most exquisite sexual thrill, yet I had no desire to be with him again. I now preferred the dream of what I wanted him to be. Besides, writing a story about him was a lot safer than an actual meeting would have been.

At first I was afraid that my escape from reality might jeopardize my down-to-earth life and love. As it turned out, no dangerous chasm existed between my imaginings and my real experiences. Rather, a meandering stream of consciousness carried my stories back into my life like water into the ocean. Behind the exotic mask of a leopard, for example, I discovered the familiar face of my husband of twenty-five years.

The moment I saw EROTICA! emblazoned in bold letters on Nell's kitchen calendar, I was hooked. What was my friend up to? I had to know! Nell invited me to the next meeting, and after eagerly accepting, I rushed home to write EROTICA! on my own calendar.

It is now nearly six years later, and I still pepper my calendar each month with EROTICA! The word stares back at me from a schedule overflowing with the usual events that are as unerotic as anything can be, but seeing EROTICA! reminds me to stop and notice, to revive and savor the sensuality that gets trampled in the haste of everyday life.

I write erotica to celebrate the ordinary. Being near-sighted, I happen to notice things closer to me and find great potential for lust and excitement in whatever finally comes into focus. Often a ludicrous discrepancy exists between reality and my perception of it, but this results less from myopia than from my expectations that so often eclipse actual events. The interplay between fantasy and reality colors my life as much as my stories.

After so much time with the Kensington Ladies, I notice that my more respectable friends and relatives are growing restless. They had expected me to outgrow this fling with erotica or, at least, to hide it in the closet where it belongs and to get on with more important pursuits. To spare them further discomfort and embarrassment, I have adopted a pseudonym whose origin I enjoy so much that I must tell it.

Long ago, in a tender moment, when I and my husband-to-be were still very new to each other, I whispered to him that his ears smelled like roast almonds.

Like a man accused, he spun around and cried out: "ROSE SOLOMON?"

"Who's *she*?" I demanded—equally alarmed.

Ever since, Rose Solomon has represented that terrible "other woman," and it seems only right that she should speak in these pages for the other me.

I am the product of an uneasy alliance between the Welsh and the French. I was born in England and educated in France, Senegal (in what was then French West Africa), and England, so by the age of four I could speak three languages. Unfortunately, I never learned the alphabet in any of them, and to this day I consult dictionaries only when no one else is around. Despite this drawback, I have been writing since the age of nine. I love words and tend to get a little out of control when writing them down on paper, as Rose and Elvira know to their editorial chagrin. (I don't care too much for rules either, except for the one about split infinitives, which I now learn to my surprise no longer matters in America.)

I joined the Kensington Ladies' Erotica Society at its second meeting. I was thrilled to join a writing group because there is always so much yeast in the atmosphere when more than one person is engaged creatively at the same time, and I was drawn by the context—EROTICA. Sabina had crystallized the vague discontent, the fretful, petulant, cloudy subthought that I had dragged around by the foot like a doll in the dust ever since I started reading modern literature in my mid teens—the feeling that *something is wrong here* when I read virile red-blooded prose. When I first met the Kensington Ladies, I was writing a series of prose-poetry pieces that dealt with my relationships to God, men, and my mother, and the phrase "God and His Brothers" kept creeping in. I have a great deal of respect for the unconscious: I assume that these gentlemen were my silencers and my judges.

So I joined Sabina and Nell and Judy and Jenna that evening in Judy's airy house high in the Kensington hills. I remember a fire and soft couches and a breathtaking view of the bay. I also remember a feeling of shyness, which we all shared at that stage, as we struggled to find our voices. What was it we wanted to say exactly? What was at stake if we said it? Was it acceptable to write autobiographically? Would the outcome be reward or punishment? God and His Brothers were out there in the sparkling dark, shadowboxing.

We shrieked a lot, I remember. We laughed a lot, too. Somebody wept. (Was it me?) Judy served a marvelous thick soup. There was a feeling both of release and of tension: some break was going to be made, some Bastille stormed. Visions of slightly tipsy pioneer women, sunbonnets askew, holding off bears and astonished Indians with a kitchen chair, wove jerkily about my consciousness like an old silent movie. What was erotica, anyway?

By the end of the evening I knew what we were about: we were claiming joint ownership of the human condition, refuting the male monopoly of sexual fantasy. It was an exhilarating, terrifying, and liberating experience. But I still find when I am patiently explaining to a strident man the difference between pornography—insidiously maiming all it touches—and erotica, which is joyful, pervasive, and utterly life-affirming, that if I turn my head a fraction over my shoulder, I can see God and His brothers wagging admonishing fingers.

I was nurtured in the lazy heat of a San Joaquin Valley vineyard. My erotic roots grow deep in California soil—sun, water, oak trees, and the dusty gold of rolling hills. Being primitive and part of nature are my earliest and most delightful memories. In rural life, time can hold quite still. I have frozen images that carry over into my writing: the triumph my six-year-old girlfriend and I felt as our photo was snapped, our toes clutching the sand of an irrigation ditch, cold water lapping at our ankles, and a blazing sun browning our bare midriffs. Being early liberated ladies, we had persuaded our mothers to buy us boy's swimming trunks, and we felt the world envied us standing there stripped to the waist, glorying in our symbolic freedom. It's only natural that I should want to continue this fun.

The erotica group was formed to explore women's true feelings as opposed to men's notions of how we felt. Our writing expressed ideas and feelings each member considered to have erotic appeal. To my chagrin I found that it was difficult, even in such congenial surroundings, to avoid the constant lament: "Well, *I* don't think that's erotic!" Obviously, there are great individual differences. In the end I decided to be myself and write about my feelings, so my stories and poems are very personal and I felt very erotic when I wrote them.

VIII. A PROPOSAL

For you, dear Reader...

If the idea of an Erotica Society appeals to you, why not form one of your own? All you have to do is whisper "Erotica" at parties, at work, and even at home, and kindred spirits will reveal themselves. Once you have aroused the curiosity of enough pleasure seekers, set a date and inscribe the word Erotica on your kitchen calendar. The magic of this word is powerful. The mixed reactions of friends and family will be the first test of your resolve to follow through. Invite your fledgling group to your house and ask each one to bring something enticing to eat or drink. Good food and wine create a safe ambiance that allows you to take the first step into the erotic unknown.

There is a huge gap between wishing and doing so don't despair if only half of your seemingly enthusiastic supporters actually appear on the chosen day. If those who do come fall silent or chatter nervously about everything but erotica, it is up to you, the hostess, to bolster them. Allow for enough small talk to get acquainted but don't get diverted. Assure the faint-hearted that nothing personal need be divulged and that whatever they reveal can be accepted as wild fabrication.

During dinner, read a story aloud from Ladies' Own Erotica. This tactic will ease your guests into the topic of the evening. Ask your listeners whether they found the story a turn-on. If not, together you can play with it to make it more erotic. Treat it like a stew. What will make it tastier— more spice? more thickening? more meat? Before you realize it, you will be making up your own tales, and your Erotica Society will be launched.

At your monthly Erotica meetings, leave the good housekeeper, mother, and job-holder behind and come as the playful child. The erotic spring is buried deep inside us beneath the rubble of childhood taboos, cultural stereotyping, and lifelong inhibitions. When you feel the urge to write, concentrate on the erotic mood you want to create. Don't rush it. Give in to chaos for a while and free your self-indulgent spirit.

Having unlocked Pandora's box, let the others have a peek. Whoever is most daring among you can be the first to read aloud. You may prefer, as we did, to hear your story read by someone else. Hearing your words is a fascinating experience, especially in the voice of a good reader. It is important to listen with empathy, to show enthusiasm, and to be lavish with your encouragement. Don't worry at this point about syntax or style. Nothing is more damaging to the erotic spirit than a lesson in English composition. Not everyone will want to write, and that is fine. Lively and responsive listening is vital. After all, you are doing this for fun.

To strengthen your conspiracy of self-indulgence, go on an erotic retreat together, even if only for a day. The farther away you are from the distractions of home, the closer you come to your erotic self. If we have learned anything from our long journey together, it is that the most erotic story of all is the one waiting to be told.

Bon voyage!
The Kensington Ladies

We would like to hear from you.
Please write to us care of Ten Speed Press,
Box 7123, Berkeley, California 94707.
The Kensington Ladies Erotica Society